HOMETOWN HEARTS

Hometown Honey

KARA LENNOX

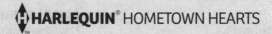

HARLEQUIN® HOMETOWN HEARTS

Recycling programs
for this product may
not exist in your area.

ISBN-13: 978-0-373-21481-5

Hometown Honey

Copyright © 2005 by Karen Leabo

This edition published by arrangement with Harlequin Books S.A.

For questions and comments about the quality of this book, please contact us at CustomerService@Harlequin.com.

Printed in U.S.A.

Kara Lennox has earned her living at various times as an art director, typesetter, textbook editor and reporter. She's worked in a boutique, a health club and an ad agency. She's been an antiques dealer, an artist and even a blackjack dealer. But no work has ever made her happier than writing romance novels. She has written more than sixty books. Kara is a recent transplant to Southern California. When not writing, she indulges in an ever-changing array of hobbies. Her latest passions are bird-watching, long-distance bicycling, vintage jewelry and, by necessity, do-it-yourself home renovation. She loves to hear from readers. You can find her at www.karalennox.com.

For Pam and the crew at Norma's Café. Your biscuits are the true inspiration for the "Miracle Biscuits." I have worked out the details of many a story sitting at one of your red vinyl booths, sucking down coffee from a bottomless cup.

Chapter One

"Only twelve thousand biscuits left to bake," Cindy Lefler said cheerfully as she popped a baking sheet into the industrial oven at the Miracle Café. Though she loved the smell of fresh-baked biscuits, she had grown weary of the actual baking. One time, she'd tried to figure out how many biscuits she'd baked in her twenty-eight years. It had numbered well into the millions.

"I wish you'd stop counting them down," grumbled Tonya Dewhurst, who was folding silverware into paper napkins. She was the café's newest waitress, but Cindy had grown to depend on her very quickly. "You're the only one who's happy you're leaving."

"I'll come back to visit."

"You'll be too busy being Mrs. Dex Shalimar, lady of leisure," Tonya said dreamily. "You sure know how to pick husbands." Then she straightened. "Oh, gosh. I didn't mean that the way it sounded."

Cindy patted Tonya's shoulder. "It's okay, I know what you mean."

She still felt a pang over losing Jim, which was only natural, she told herself. The disagreement between her husband's truck and a freight train had happened only a year ago. But she *had* picked a good one when she'd married him. And she'd gotten just plain lucky finding Dex.

"It's almost six," Cindy said. "Would you unlock the front door and turn on the Open sign, please?" A couple of the other waitresses, Iris and Kate, had arrived and were going through their morning routines. Iris had worked at the café for more than twenty years, Kate almost as long.

Tonya smiled. "Sure. Um, Cindy, do you have a buyer for the café yet?"

"Dex says he has some serious nibbles."

"I just hope the new owner will let me bring Micton to work with me."

Cindy cringed every time she heard that name. Tonya had thought it was so cute naming her baby with a combination of hers and her husband's names—Mick and Tonya. Micton. Yikes! It was the type of backwoods logic that made Cindy want to leave Cottonwood.

Customers were actually waiting in line when Tonya opened the door—farmers and ranchers, mostly, in jeans and overalls, Stetsons and gimme hats, here to get a hearty breakfast and exchange gossip. Cindy went to work on the Daily Specials chalkboard, suspended high above the cash register.

"'Morning, Ms. Cindy."

She very nearly fell off her stepladder. Still, she managed to call out a very pleasant, "'Morning, Luke." The handsome sheriff's deputy always unnerved her. He showed up at 6:10 a.m., like clockwork, five days a week, and ordered the same thing—one biscuit with honey and black coffee. But every single time she saw him sitting there at the counter, that knowing grin on his face, she felt a flutter of surprise.

Kate rushed over from clearing a table to pour Luke his coffee and take his order. The woman was in her sixties. at least, but Cindy could swear Kate blushed as she served Luke. He just had that effect on women, herself included. Even now, when she was engaged—hell, even when she'd been *married* to a man she'd loved fiercely—just looking at Luke made her pulse quicken and her face warm.

She refused to blame herself. It was just hormones. The man was sexier than the devil himself, with that curly chestnut hair and those eyes, green and dark as a cool, mossy pond. In high school, he'd worn his hair long and unruly, sometimes past his shoulders, as part of his go-to-hell image. He'd made girls drool back then when he was still a skinny teenager. He'd inspired Cindy to do a lot more than drool. Now, with that uniform and the wide shoulders to fill it out and the hair cut shorter in a futile attempt to tame it, he was even more mouthwatering.

"So, how are the wedding plans coming along?" Luke asked Cindy. A bystander might assume the question was borne of polite curiosity, but Cindy knew better. Luke Rheems had despised Dexter Shalimar on sight, and he never missed an opportunity to subtly remind Cindy that he thought she was a fool for marrying Dex.

"There aren't many plans for me to make," Cindy said breezily. "Dex is handling all the arrangements. We're flying to Lake Tahoe, getting married in a little chapel in the mountains and then Dex is going to teach me to ski." It was the sort of vacation she'd always dreamed of. She and Jim had visited Lake Tahoe before, of course. She'd gasped at the breathtaking scenery, the opulent homes, the flashy casinos. But there'd been no money for skiing or gambling, and they'd slept either in their truck or at a cheap motel.

This time, her honeymoon would be four-star hotels, fancy meals, private skiing lessons.

"Dex handles a lot for you, doesn't he? The sale of your restaurant and your house, your wedding, your honeymoon. He's chosen where you'll live—"

"Dex is in real estate," Cindy broke in, climbing down from the stepladder. She couldn't spell and argue with Luke at the same time. "Why shouldn't he handle my real-estate transactions? It's what he's good at. As for our home, yes, he did pick it out and furnish it. But I'm no good at decorating—he hired an expert to do that. Anyway, I've seen it and it's perfect. A no-fuss penthouse with all maintenance taken care of."

"And no backyard. Where will Adam play?"

She lowered her voice, getting truly irritated. "Don't you start laying that guilt trip on me. My son is going to have a fabulous childhood. Dex has business all over the globe, so we'll all travel the world together. Adam will meet and play with children of all cultures. He'll frolic in alpine meadows and on Jamaican beaches. He'll sample fresh foods from Italy and Indonesia. You act like he'll be deprived simply because he doesn't have a postage stamp of grass to call his own."

"I happen to believe a child *does* need a few blades of grass to call his own."

"And when you have a child of your own, you can raise him in a little backyard like a rabbit in his hutch. With the same view, seeing the same people, eating the same foods day in and day out." She knew she should stop there, but he'd hit her hot button. "And he'll grow up to be just as closed-minded and provincial as everybody else in this town, afraid of anything that's strange or foreign or the slightest bit different."

Luke arched one eyebrow at her, surprised by her outburst. "Is that how you see your Cottonwood neighbors? A bunch of ignorant, closed-minded xenophobes?"

Cindy was embarrassed to admit she didn't know what *xenophobe* meant. But that was part of her point—and part of why she wanted something different for Adam. Sure, she'd traveled the country, but she'd never been to college. She wasn't well read. She didn't know anything about stylish clothes or entertaining or even how to fix her hair, which was currently pulled back in a loose ponytail. Dex had never criticized, but if she was going to be the wife of a high-society millionaire, she was going to have to work on her shortcomings.

To mask her ignorance, she changed the subject. "You're just raining on my parade because you're jealous."

"Jealous? Oh, yeah, right. Of Dex? He's a pencil-neck weenie."

"Now you are obviously desperate, resorting to name-calling. By the way, I never heard the results of your big investigation into Dex's background. You were going to uncover all his terrible secrets, right? The three other wives, the jail time, the sixteen illegitimate children?"

At least Luke had the good grace to look slightly ashamed. "He checked out," was all he said.

As Cindy had known he would. She hadn't just fallen off the turnip truck yesterday. She'd done a little checking of her own. Dexter Shalimar, though notoriously publicity wary and camera shy, was considered Houston's hottest bachelor and one of its richest residents. His company, Shalimar Holdings, was one of the largest privately owned real-estate-development companies in the nation and one of the few that didn't take a terrible beating during the recent recession. He'd never been married, had no children, had never been arrested. He was a major contributor to several charities and had come in seventeenth last year in the Boston Marathon. What was not to like?

As to whether she loved him—well, that was another matter. Jim would always occupy a very special place in her heart, and he couldn't be shoved aside. But she was very, very fond of Dex, Adam seemed to adore him and she knew of many strong marriages based on mutual respect and affection.

Luke finished his biscuit and took his coffee in a to-go cup, as always. At about seven-thirty, the town-square business owners started arriving. Then, a little later, the moms who'd gotten their kids off to school showed up, along with the retirees. The breakfast trade had hardly let up before the early lunch crowd started trickling in.

It was a good, busy morning. But then, the café had always been a moneymaker. An unofficial historic landmark, it had supported Cindy's family comfortably for generations. Still, Cindy had never felt any real attachment to the business. She'd worked here evenings and weekends and summers since she could remember, with the exception of the eight years she'd traveled the country with Jim in his 18-wheeler. To her, the Miracle Café meant turning down every other opportunity that had come her way—cheerleading, drama club, soccer. Her parents had worked twelve-hour days, seven days a week, and she'd been expected to follow suit.

The workload had only gotten worse since her mother's death. As the sole owner, Cindy found it nearly impossible to take a long weekend, much less ramble around the country.

Now that she had Adam, she thought as she transferred a selection of meringue pies from cooling racks in the kitchen to the glass-fronted bakery case out front, the café was even more confining. She brought the baby to work with her, as Tonya did, where all the waitresses and even the busboys took turns spoiling him. But Cindy herself was so busy, she didn't feel as if she spent enough time with him.

That would all change in a couple of months, she thought with a warm glow. She would travel from one adventure to another, the way she'd always dreamed. And once she and Dex were married, she was going to travel with him—she and Adam. She'd seen a lot of her own country before Jim's death. Now, the world would be her oyster.

"Cindy?" It was Tonya, a water pitcher in one hand, menus in the other. "Those two ladies in booth three want to speak to you."

Cindy glanced over to the booth by the window. In it sat two women, both blond, both obviously not from Cottonwood. One was dressed in a business suit, her artfully highlighted hair twisted into a complicated configuration atop her head. The other had really funky, spiky, frosted hair and an abundance of silver jewelry.

Could be a real-estate agent and her client, she thought optimistically. Cindy smoothed her apron, wiped her hands on a towel and, with a parting glance at Luke that told him to stop messing with her, she approached the women.

"Hello," she said brightly. "I'm Cindy Lefler, owner of the Miracle Café." She stretched her hand out in greeting to the one in the business suit.

The other woman squeezed her hand briefly. She didn't smile. "Sonya Patterson. And this is Brenna Thompson. Please, could you sit down?" She indicated the red vinyl banquette across from her.

Cindy sat next to the one called Brenna, feeling apprehensive. "What can I do for you?"

Sonya set a leather briefcase on the table and snapped open the locks. She withdrew a color photo and slid it across the table toward Cindy. "Do you know this man?"

The photo was a bit blurry, as if it had been blown up. Clearly the man in the picture had had his arm around someone else, who'd been cropped out.

"Of course. That's my fiancé, Dexter Shalimar," Cindy said tightly.

Sonya's eyes seemed to grow brighter and Brenna sat forward slightly. "The real-estate tycoon?" Brenna asked. "*That* Dexter Shalimar?"

"Yes. Is it so unbelievable that he would want to marry a waitress?"

Neither woman answered Cindy's question. Instead Sonya asked, "Do you know where he is? Right this moment, I mean?"

"Not that it's any of your business, but he's in Malaysia on a business trip. Look, what is this about?" Cindy had an unpleasant crawly sensation at the back of her neck.

Sonya sank back in her seat. "Oh, I hope I'm not too late."

"Too late for what?"

"I don't know how to tell you this except to just blurt it out. The man in that photo is not Dexter Shalimar. His name is Marvin Carter and he's a con man."

Cindy's face grew hot. "I don't know who you think you are or what you're trying to pull, but Dexter Shalimar is no con man. Would a con man give a woman a ring like this?" She always tucked her three-carat engagement ring into her pocket while she was working. She pulled it out now and flashed the enormous pear-shaped diamond under Sonya's nose.

Sonya gave the ring a perfunctory glance. "Hmm. It looks a lot like mine." She reached into her purse and pulled out a ring that was identical to Cindy's.

"And mine." Brenna opened her leather backpack and also produced a similar ring.

"I assume you haven't had it appraised," Sonya said. "It's a cubic zirconia. Worth about twenty-eight bucks. I think he buys them by the gross."

"I don't believe you," Cindy said flatly. "He

is Dex Shalimar. He drives a Porsche 911. He's just bought us a million-dollar penthouse. I've been there."

"Oh, the penthouse on Riva Row?" asked Sonya. "That would be *my* penthouse. Or it used to be mine, until he sold it out from under me, pocketed the cash and skipped town."

Cindy's head was beginning to buzz. This couldn't be true—it just couldn't be. "I want you to leave," Cindy said frostily.

"Of course." Sonya flashed her a sympathetic smile. "I know how hard this is, believe me. But check your bank accounts. If there's still any money in them, count yourself lucky. And change your account numbers."

Sonya slid out of the booth. Brenna scrambled after her. They both looked at Cindy sadly, as if she were a puppy they were leaving behind at the dog pound. Then they left the café, Sonya's heels tapping on the linoleum floor.

Cindy just sat there. Should she try to get in touch with Dex, tell him two mad women were running around maligning him? He'd said he would be out of touch. But surely his company would know how to contact him.

Then an awful, alien thought stirred in her brain. She should call the bank. Just to be sure.

Someone scooted into the booth across from

her. She looked up to see Luke Rheems, his handsome face etched with concern. "Cindy? You okay? Who were those women?"

"Yes, I'm fine. Of course I'm fine. Why wouldn't I be fine? And those women are nut-cases. You should keep an eye on them, Luke. They're up to no good." Then she stood up and made a hasty escape before her panic took control of her and she started screaming.

Keeping her gaze straight ahead, not acknowledging any customers' or employees' looks of concern, she headed for her office and slipped inside. Both Adam and Micton were napping, thank heavens. Micton was still tiny and slept most of the time, anyway. Adam, however, had just turned fourteen months, and he was getting more active by the minute. Soon he would be too much to handle at work, and she would have to find a full-time babysitter.

She paused a moment to watch her son sleeping, his thumb in his mouth, his favorite blanky clutched in his other hand. He was the light of her life. She'd never expected to enjoy motherhood. But she'd taken to it like a hog to mud, proving that she did in fact have at least one domestic bone in her body, contrary to what her parents had always said.

Enough distraction. She had to call the bank.

And then, when she heard everything was as it should be, she could laugh off her momentary worries.

Cindy found the number in her Rolodex, then dialed. She asked for her personal banker, Mary Dietz.

"Oh, hi, Cindy. It's nice to hear from you. How can I help you?"

Cindy made her request to check the balance in her checking account. It was exactly where it should be, seven hundred and change. She breathed a little easier.

"And my money-market fund?"

There was a long silence. "That account is closed."

"No, you're thinking of my mother's account. I closed that out last year when her estate was settled. I'm talking about my personal savings account. Here's the number." She rattled off the long account number.

Another long silence. "Cindy, Mr. Shalimar closed that account last week. I handled it personally. He said you were investing the funds into real estate."

That buzz was starting up in Cindy's head again. "Are you sure?" But she knew that was a stupid question. Mary didn't make mistakes.

"Oh, my gosh, of course," Cindy said, masking her panic as best she could. "I forgot he was going to do that. Okay, never mind. Sorry I bothered you." She hung up.

Could it possibly be true, what those women had told her? That Dex wasn't Dex at all, but someone named Marvin who'd given her a fake ring, shown her a penthouse that wasn't even his and made off with close to three-quarters of a million dollars—Jim's entire life-insurance benefit, her parents' life savings and both her and Jim's savings?

She picked up the phone again, frantically dialing Dex's cell number. She got a recording that the number wasn't valid. She dialed again, thinking she must have misdialed in her haste. But she got the same result.

On a mission now, she pulled the Houston phone book from her bottom desk drawer and looked up the number for Shalimar Holdings. Dex had always told her not to bother calling him at the office, where she would have to wade through layers of receptionists and secretaries to get to him. His cell was always on, always with him and a much easier way to reach him.

She dialed the business number, reached a secretary. "This is an emergency. I really, really need to get word to Dexter Shalimar. Does he have an assistant or someone I could talk to?"

"May I ask who's calling?"

"This is Cindy Lefler, his fiancée. I know he's in Malaysia, but surely you people have a way of getting through to him in an emergency?"

Long silence. "Mr. Shalimar is not in Malaysia. Nor does he have a fiancée named Cindy or anything else. Shall I transfer your call to security?"

Cindy couldn't speak. She simply hung up the phone.

She had to get out of here, go home, pull herself together. She couldn't let her customers or employees see her falling apart. She couldn't let anyone know what was happening until she'd figured it out for herself.

She packed up Adam's diaper bag and her purse and car keys, then gently picked up Adam from his playpen. He stirred slightly, then opened his eyes and blinked blearily at her.

She cuddled him against her shoulder. Thank goodness he wasn't a cranky baby. He was very adaptable, willing to sleep anywhere, eat anything, play with whatever was on hand, allow anyone to hold him. He would be a fabulous traveling companion, she'd told herself many times.

She ducked into the kitchen long enough to tell her cook, Manson Grable, that she was going home because she didn't feel well.

"Is there anything I can do?" Manson asked. He was sixty, portly, round faced and had worked for the Miracle Café his whole adult life. "Can I send you home with some chicken soup?"

"I'll be fine—just a headache." She forced a smile and had almost made it out the back door when a booming voice from the dining room snagged her attention.

"I'm looking for Cindy Lefler!"

She considered escaping, then decided it might be important. With a heavy heart, she walked back through the kitchen and out the swinging doors into the dining room.

Standing in the middle of the dining room, looking something like King Henry VIII in madras shorts, a Hawaiian shirt and flip-flops, was the man who'd spoken.

"Hi, I'm Cindy Lefler," Cindy said, lacking her usual smiling hospitality. "Can I help you?"

"I'm Ed LaRue."

She looked at him blankly. The name meant nothing to her.

"I'm the new owner of the Miracle Café," he continued, still grinning. "Soon to be Ed's Enchilada Emporium!"

Chapter Two

Deputy Luke Rheems looked at first one, then the other of the two women seated in his office. They were both attractive, but beyond their blond hair, they were complete opposites. Sonya Patterson was the epitome of wealth and sophistication. Tall and slim with an elegant, aristocratic face, she wore an ivory linen suit, sheer stockings that looked like silk and cream-colored leather pumps with a medium heel. Her nails were long, probably acrylic, and salon fresh with a coating of pale pink-frosted polish. Her artfully highlighted hair was piled atop her head in a complicated twist, not a strand out of place.

Brenna Thompson was petite, with a pleasantly curvaceous figure, and she looked as if she belonged in an artist's loft in SoHo. Her platinum-frosted hair was short and spiky, sticking out of her head like a porcupine's quills, and her eye shadow was a particularly virulent shade of purple. Her left ear was graced with five piercings, each with a distinctly unique silver earring.

The rest of her jewelry was just as interesting, and she wore a lot of it—rings on almost every finger, bracelets jangling with every movement of her arms, a handful of chains around her neck from which dangled charms in whimsical animal shapes, their eyes winking with colored stones. Her snug, tie-dyed T-shirt didn't quite meet up with her faded hip-hugger jeans, leaving a couple of inches of strategically exposed flesh at her midriff. Though she was categorically not his type, she exuded healthy sex appeal.

"We're starting to get worried about her," Sonya was saying. "After we broke the news to her that her supposed fiancée was—"

"Lying, thieving pond scum," Brenna supplied.

"Yes, exactly. After that, she got the news

that her restaurant had been sold out from under her."

"It must have been too much," Brenna said. "She's gone into hiding."

"We understand she hasn't come out of her house in days," Sonya continued. "Now, we hardly know Cindy, but we know what it feels like to have the rug pulled out from underneath you. We figured she needed some time to grieve and we've left her alone. But, Deputy Rheems, it's been almost a week and she hasn't come out of her house. She won't answer the phone or the doorbell. We're worried about her."

Luke had been worried about Cindy, too. He'd left the Miracle Café just minutes before Ed LaRue's dramatic arrival, so he hadn't witnessed it. But he'd heard through the grapevine about it—and that it was all true. Dexter Shalimar, aka Marvin Carter, had sold the Miracle Café, and the sale was more or less legal because Cindy had signed some power-of-attorney paper giving her fiancé the right to conduct all sorts of business for her.

Every suspicion he'd harbored about Cindy's boyfriend had been right on the money. The man was a liar, a thief, a con man, a snake. The only thing Luke had missed was that Shalimar wasn't Shalimar at all. He'd borrowed the reclusive real-estate tycoon's identity. Luke should have suspected that. But when his initial inquiries into Shalimar's background had checked out, he'd had no legitimate reason to snoop any further, so he hadn't.

After the manure hit the fan, Luke had tried to call Cindy a couple of times to see if she wanted to press charges. He'd managed to get her on the phone once; she'd brushed him off with a quick, insincere assurance that she was fine, everything was fine—it was all a misunderstanding.

But as his visitors had pointed out, no one had seen her or Adam in almost a week.

"I'll go to her house, see how she's doing," Luke said.

"Please tell her we need to meet with her," Brenna said. "We need her help if we're going to catch this guy."

"Now, ladies, I understand your anger and frustration, but I think you'd better let the law-enforcement authorities handle—"

"Oh, yeah, right," Brenna interrupted. "If Marvin happens to walk into the House of Donuts and identify himself, maybe the cops'll stop him. But I wouldn't count on even that. So far they sent out a couple of faxes, put his name on a list somewhere and went back to sleep."

"The law-enforcement people don't care," Sonya agreed. "Marvin hasn't murdered anyone. He's not a bigamist, since he doesn't actually marry his victims. He's small potatoes to them. But not to us, and not to the next woman he'll go after. And believe me, he isn't going to stop. It might be too late to get our money back, but we're going to make him pay in ways he never dreamed of."

"Never underestimate the power of a woman scorned," Brenna added, sharing a look of solidarity with Sonya.

Luke decided he'd rather have Bubba the Bounty Hunter on his trail than these two. They suddenly seemed a little scary to him.

As Luke drove his SUV down Cindy's street, his stomach did a little flutter. It was the same little flutter he got every time he walked into the Miracle Café for his morning coffee and biscuit. And it was Cindy Lefler who did it to him.

He'd been crazy in love with her at one time. Cindy's naive adoration of him, her pure, uncomplicated emotions, her gentle ways, had gone a long way toward healing the abandoned little boy inside him, and he'd never forgotten it. But she'd been appalled when, just after high school graduation he'd suggested they get married and settle down. That was before he'd realized *settle down* were dirty words to Cindy.

It wasn't long after that when long-haul trucker Jim Lefler had stopped for lunch at the Miracle Café and had become entranced with his young waitress, and she with him. Three weeks later, they'd eloped.

When Adam had come along and they'd bought a house in Cottonwood, Jim had fit right in, and everyone agreed that they made a terrific family.

Even Luke came to like Jim Lefler. His unexpected death was an awful thing, and Luke had mourned the passing of a friend and an essential member of the community.

But then there was Cindy, alone again and apparently here in Cottonwood to stay. Luke had promised himself he would wait at least a year before even flirting with Cindy. Then that jerk Dexter Shalimar—Marvin Carter, he reminded himself—had shown up, taking advantage of a woman not only grieving for her husband but her mother, who'd passed not long after Jim. Luke's timing had always been bad when it came to Cindy.

Luke pulled in to the driveway of the tidy little three-bedroom house Jim and Cindy had bought. The grass needed mowing, he noted, and the flower beds were full of weeds. The blinds were drawn.

Before going to the front door, he peeked through a window into the garage. Cindy's car was there. He felt a prickle of unease.

He climbed the three stairs to the front porch and rang the bell. He could hear a TV inside, then a child's babble. Adam was okay, at least. But Cindy didn't answer the door.

He knocked loudly. "Cindy? It's me, Luke. I know you're in there, so open the door."

"I'm busy, Luke," she finally called through the door. "You'll have to come back another time."

"I need to talk to you."

"Why?"

"Would you just for heaven's sake open the door?"

He heard her unfasten the chain, then crack the door. "What is it?"

He could see only half her face. Her wavy, honey-colored hair hung limply to her shoulders. Her complexion was too pale.

He couldn't see much of the rest of her, just her shoulder and arm and one leg. She wore faded gray sweatpants and a T-shirt with the Red Dog Saloon logo on it.

She was allowed to look a little grubby, he told himself. But her lack of grooming bothered him.

"How are you doing?" he asked gently. "Everyone's worried about you."

"Why? I'm… I'm fine. I'm just very busy. Making wedding plans, you know. I have to pack—"

"Cindy, give it a rest. You're not getting married. Dexter or Marvin or whoever he is isn't coming back now that he's got your money. You've been had by a very slick, very convincing con man. The best thing is for you to face what's happened head-on."

"Does everyone know?" she asked in a whisper.

"Everyone knows, and everyone wants to help any way they can."

"Oh, my God." She turned away from the door but left it open. Luke took the opportunity to follow her inside.

The sight that greeted him was alarming, to say the least. The living room was a wreck, littered with empty pizza boxes, dirty dishes, toys, blankets and stacks of videotapes. The sofa cushions were on the floor. It looked as if Cindy had been sleeping in front of the TV.

He would never have classified Cindy as compulsively neat, but normally she wasn't slovenly, either.

"Looks like you've been in some kind of funk, girl."

Cindy did not want to see Luke Rheems, of all people. He'd warned her about Dex. His lawman's instincts had picked up on qualities Cindy had missed because of her stupid, blind adoration of a man who had pretended to be everything she was looking for. Seeing Luke made her feel even worse, if that was possible.

She wished he would just go away. If everyone would leave her alone, she would be fine.

"I'm merely taking this opportunity to spend some quiet time with my son," she said, mustering as much dignity as she could.

Luke went around the living room and dining room opening the blinds.

"It's like a cave in here. And it doesn't smell too good, either." He opened a couple of windows. "There."

"What sort of rumors have those two women been spreading?"

"They haven't talked to anyone but me, as

far as I know. But, Cindy, it's obvious to everyone what's happened. Ed LaRue is not a quiet man. Apparently Marvin Carter made up all kinds of lies about you, the town and the café. LaRue is repeating them."

"Is the café still open?" Cindy asked. She'd been afraid to call or drive by.

"No. Ed closed it up and fired all the employees. He has an extended family he plans to give full employment to."

"Oh, no. Poor Kate and Iris and Tonya—and Manson! What will they do?"

"What will *you* do?"

"I'm fine. I was going to sell the restaurant anyway. I'll be happy not to ever bake another biscuit as long as I live."

"You're not fine, Cindy. If Marvin Carter followed his usual MO, he wiped you out." He took her by the arms and looked straight into her eyes. "C'mon, honey, snap out of it. You have to do something. You have to take action. It's not just you anymore. You have a child to support."

"Adam is being well taken care of, thank you very much." She shook off Luke's touch, though in truth it was tempting to just fall into those strong arms, to lean against Luke's muscular shoulder and cry her little eyes out.

"Okay, maybe Dexter's…unexpected and inappropriate actions have knocked me a little off balance. But I'm taking good care of Adam." She'd bathed him every day, even if she'd been less scrupulous about her own grooming, and he always got clean clothes and three healthy meals a day.

Instead of believing her, Luke walked into her kitchen, past more piles of dirty dishes and empty cereal boxes and milk bottles, and opened the fridge.

"It looks a little meager."

"I need to go to the store. Big deal."

"And how will you pay for the groceries?"

"I have money." But not as much as she'd thought. The seven hundred-plus dollars in her checking account had dwindled down to under two hundred once her last mortgage check had cleared. She'd figured she could afford another week's worth of groceries—another week she could pretend that Dex was coming back.

Luke looked at her, his disbelief evident in those deep, knowing eyes of his.

"I've got lots of equity in my house. I can get an equity loan to tide me over while I regroup."

"I hope you're right."

The *chug-chugging* of a diesel engine reverberated outside, coming to a pause in front of

Cindy's house. Curious, she returned to the living room and looked out the window. A huge Ryder truck was in the process of backing over her lawn, the rear headed directly for her front porch.

"Oh, my—" She ran out the front door and up to the truck's cab, beating on the driver's door.

The window slid down and Ed LaRue was behind the wheel, grinning ear to ear. "Well, hi, there, sweet thing. Thought you'd be long gone to your new house in San Francisco."

"What do you think you're doing?" Cindy sputtered. But she knew. Oh, Lord, she knew. Dex—Marvin, dammit—had sold her house, too. She was not only penniless, she was homeless. Next thing she knew, the insufferable Ed LaRue would claim her car.

Luke convinced LaRue to give Cindy another twenty-four hours to clear out of her house. To seal the deal, he pulled out his wallet and handed Ed a wad of cash. "Dinner's on me, okay?"

Slightly mollified, Ed took the money. "I'll agree to this, you being a lawman and all. But this house by God, better be empty by tomorrow morning, or there'll be hell to pay."

He closed the window and the truck lumbered out of the front yard and down the street.

Cindy just looked at Luke. "You didn't have to do that."

"I want to help. That's the main reason I got this job, you know. To help people. To resolve conflicts."

"How much did you give him? I'll pay you back."

"Don't worry about that. The main thing is I bought you a little time, but not much. I get off at three and I can get a horse trailer from my brother's place and help you move."

Where? Where was she going to move? She'd sold her parents' house. She had no other relatives in the area. She couldn't possibly move in on Tonya or Kate or Iris—they had enough trouble, what with their sudden unemployment and all.

But she couldn't admit her dire straits to Luke. He was the one who'd warned her about Dex—Marvin, dammit. She was so humiliated, felt so stupid, and she just couldn't bear to rely on his kind, compassionate help a moment longer.

Plus, she was going to have an emotional crash. She'd been holding back a colossal crying jag for days, and she didn't want him to witness that.

"I do have a place to go," she said. "And I'm not going to worry about moving furniture. It's all garage-sale stuff anyway—let Ed LaRue have it. I'll take our clothes and a few personal items, nothing that won't fit in my car trunk. I appreciate your offer to help, Luke—I really do. But I'll be fine."

He looked as if he didn't believe her.

She forced a smile and made shooing motions with her hands. "Run along. Go catch some criminals. I have a little packing to do."

"If I find out you're lying about this, I'm coming after you," he threatened. "Call me when you're settled someplace."

"Sure." When hell froze over.

"Oh, and you need to contact those women— Brenna and Sonya?"

She sighed. "Why?" She didn't want to wallow in shared stupidity with these other women, women who'd loved Dex or whatever name he'd given them, women who'd probably slept with him, who'd thought they were marrying him. "I want to move forward, not dwell on past mistakes."

"Well, they want to catch Marvin and get their money back, or at least enjoy the satisfaction of putting him behind bars. I've agreed to help them. You have the most current information on Marvin. You could help a lot."

"I'll think about it," she said, though she hadn't yet managed to summon up enough anger toward Dex/Marvin to want vengeance. She was still in disbelief with more than a hint of denial. Part of her expected Dex's familiar lemon-yellow Porsche to come hauling up the street, the trunk full of presents for her and Adam.

"Just one more thing." Without warning, he hauled her into his arms and hugged her fiercely.

"Luke!"

"Hush. You need this."

The security of his embrace, the warmth of his body, felt way better than it should have. She knew she should end it, but for a few moments, all she wanted to do was empty her mind and drown in his warmth, his caring.

She'd always been able to count on his caring. Even when she'd treated him not so nicely, back in high school, he'd had a seemingly inexhaustible ability to forgive her, even if he couldn't understand exactly what made her tick, what made her want to wander the world in search of new sights, new adventures.

After a few moments, it was Luke who loosened his arms first. She pulled back reluctantly, realizing as she did that hugging her might not be that pleasant given that she hadn't bathed in two days. "Thanks, Luke," she whispered, perilously close to tears again as she escaped inside her house.

Which wasn't really her house any longer, she reminded herself. Cindy mentally shook off her lethargy. She couldn't take refuge in inactivity any longer. She had to move, make decisions.

When she'd told Luke she had someplace to go, she'd thought she was lying. But maybe there was someplace.

Her parents had owned a boat, which was moored at Town Lake. It was an old, twenty-foot cuddy cruiser. Her father's idea had been that they would fix it up, then take it to Lake Texoma. When Cindy was little, they used to close the restaurant on holidays and spend a day or two on the lake, floating aimlessly on the water while they sanded and painted and sewed curtains. But then their interest had waned. No one had used the boat for years and Cindy had been meaning to sell it.

She'd surely never mentioned the boat to Dex. It might be the one asset he'd overlooked.

And though it was small, it had a sleeping cabin with a real bed and a tiny galley with a one-burner stove and a marine toilet. She'd recently paid for six months' dock fees at the marina.

Maybe it wasn't a great plan, but it beat sleeping in her car.

Cindy started packing. She found a few boxes and suitcases in the attic and filled them with clothes—she didn't have many—toiletries and Adam's favorite toys. She did laundry— no telling when she'd have her next chance. She loaded everything in her car, along with Adam's collapsible playpen.

Lastly, she packed up her food—every crumb. It was enough to last her a few more days. She put the stuff from the fridge in a cooler, along with some ice.

"Well, baby," she cooed to Adam, "I said I wanted adventure. Guess I should be careful what I wish for, huh?"

Adam laughed and made a grab for her earring. She was glad he was too young to understand, too young to share the insidious fear that had crept into every cell of her body.

Broke, homeless, jobless and with a child to support. What a mess she'd gotten herself into.

Chapter Three

Luke watched from a distance, lurking in the shadows at the marina behind a houseboat. He'd heard a rumor that Cindy and Adam were living here on her parents' old boat, but he had to see for himself.

Sure enough, the canvas cover had been removed from the old cuddy, which was called the Cindy-Lou—Cindy's childhood nickname. It looked as if someone had cleaned the worst of the grime off the boat. Carlo Bruno, the marina manager, had told Luke the boat had been docked here for years, with only the lightest routine maintenance to keep it from sinking.

He saw no other signs of life. He decided it

was his official duty to check on Cindy again and to keep checking on her until he was sure she was okay. She'd been in a fragile state when he'd seen her a few days ago.

He remembered a time when his own mother had been in a similar fix. He'd been about four at the time, and his mom had been evicted from her grungy apartment in Tyler. They'd been forced to live in the car for a while. He remembered a highway patrol officer shining a flashlight into the car, where they'd been parked in a parking lot trying to sleep, bundled up in blankets. And this upstanding law-enforcement officer, sworn to serve and protect, had told them without an ounce of concern that they would have to move on, that it was illegal to sleep there.

He wished someone had tried to help his mother back then, when she hadn't yet been beyond help.

At any rate, he wasn't going to be like that state trooper.

He stepped on board and knocked on the hatch. It suddenly occurred to him he'd spent a lot of his life knocking on doors, waiting for Cindy. Even when she'd been in love with him, she'd always kept him waiting.

Eventually the hatch opened. He was gratified to see that Cindy looked much better than she had a few days ago. No puffy eyes. Her hair was sparkling clean and pulled back in a loose braid, and she wore jeans and a pale pink T-shirt, the V-neck showing just a hint of cleavage. She'd put on a little weight, he noticed. And it was in all the right places.

"What are you doing here?" she asked suspiciously.

"I heard you and Adam were living here. I just wanted to see how you were doing."

"I'm fine. Everything's fine. You can tell that to all the town gossips. Man, they must be having a field day with this."

"Cindy, if you think your friends and neighbors are getting enjoyment out of your bad luck, you're wrong. Everyone who knows you is worried. Can I come in?"

With a careless shrug, she retreated down the short staircase and he followed. The boat wasn't as bad as he'd feared. She'd obviously been cleaning, because the whole place smelled like oranges.

"You want some coffee?" she offered grudgingly. "It's instant, not like what I serve at the café, but the caffeine still works."

"Sure, I'll have some. Where's Adam?"

"Still asleep. We've been busy the last couple of days trying to get settled in here."

She moved into the tiny galley, which was only a couple of steps away. In fact, nothing was more than two steps away. It was a cute and cozy boat, he'd give it that. The carpeting and upholstery all looked new, the paint surprisingly fresh. Everything was tidy and efficient—except for the stack of boxes shoved to one side of the living room.

Moments later, Cindy handed him a steaming cup of black coffee.

"What, no biscuit with honey?"

"You know, a few days ago I was complaining about all the biscuits I had to bake. Now I'd give anything to be back in that stifling kitchen with flour all over my hands."

"Maybe you can get it back."

"How? I don't even know where to start."

"To start, you need to talk with Sonya and Brenna."

"You mean they're still here?"

"They're trying to pick up as much information as they can about Marvin, but they don't have much without you."

"I'm not sure what the point is." She sank onto one of the miniature built-in sofas opposite him and sipped on her own coffee. "Everything I know about him is a lie, apparently."

"But maybe not. Con men often use bits and pieces of the truth to make themselves sound more authentic. You might know more than you think. For instance, his car. You spent a lot of time in it. Do you recall the license plate or any distinguishing features like dents or scratches? We might be able to trace him that way."

Cindy's brow furrowed. "It all seems like a blur. But I'll try to remember."

"Talk to the ladies."

"Oh, all right."

He hesitated to press her further, but there were questions he had to ask. "Cindy, what are you going to do? You can't live here."

"Why not? I have a kitchen." She pointed to the one-burner stove, a single cabinet and about one square foot of counter space. "I have a bathroom." She indicated a closed door marked Head, which probably housed only a marine toilet and sink—no bathing facilities.

"Where do you sleep?"

"There's a compartment in the bow. You can see for yourself."

"I don't want to wake Adam if he's—"

"It's really time he got up."

Luke put down his coffee and worked his way

to the front of the boat. He had to stoop slightly—
he couldn't even stand upright, the ceiling was so
low. He pushed open a couple of louvered doors
and found himself in the "bedroom"—a tiny tri-
angular area with sheets and blankets spread out
over oddly shaped cushions. Adam was already
awake, sitting up in bed, looking out the port-
hole. Most babies he knew of started screaming
the instant they awoke. But from what he'd seen
of Adam, he was an easygoing kid.

"Hey, there, sport," he said softly. Adam
turned and studied Luke, appearing neither
scared nor pleased to see him. More curious.
"I bet you're ready for some breakfast."

"Do you mind bringing him out?" Cindy
asked.

"If he'll let me." But when Luke reached for
Adam, the baby held his arms out, perfectly ac-
cepting. Not that Luke was a complete stranger.
But the baby had seen him up close maybe half
a dozen times in his young life. Luke wrapped
his arms securely around Adam's warm body,
dressed snugly in Carter's pajamas. Adam babbled happily and snuggled against Luke.

Luke felt an odd sensation holding that baby.
If things had gone the way he'd once hoped,
Cindy's child would also be *his* child. They'd
have had a houseful by now.

"There's my little man," Cindy said with a dopey, maternal smile, holding out her arms. "Bet you need a diaper change." She glanced at Luke as she took the baby. "Don't worry, I'll open some portholes first."

He laughed. "I'm not worried. You want me to get you a diaper?"

She pointed to a box of disposables and a container of baby wipes, and she proceeded to efficiently change Adam's diaper.

"Where do you bathe?" Luke blurted out. Though it sounded as if he was being nosy, this really was his business, he told himself.

"The marina has a very nice bathroom with showers and everything."

"So Adam's a shower man."

"He's learning. We shower together."

Luke didn't want to dwell on the image that popped into his mind.

"Cindy…you can't stay here."

"Why not? We're managing just fine. Anyway, it's only temporary, just until I figure out what to do."

"Does this place have any heat?"

"No. But the weather's very mild right now."

"It's October. You know the weather can change in a heartbeat."

"I'll deal with that problem when I come to it."

They were saved from further argument by another knock on the hatch. For a moment, Cindy had a look on her face that reminded Luke of a scared rabbit.

"You want me to get that?"

"Would you, please?" She was just snapping up Adam's pajamas. "And if it's those women, tell them I'll talk to them when I'm ready, not before," she added crossly.

Luke climbed the steps and unfastened the barrel bolt. He pushed the hatch outward and found himself staring into the round, brown eyes of an attractive African-American woman wearing a worn sweaterdress, white stockings and scuffed black pumps. Not exactly boating clothes.

She smiled uncertainly. "Hi, I'm Beverly Hicks. I'm looking for a Cindy Lefler?"

Alarm bells went off in Luke's head. The woman's appearance and demeanor screamed one thing to him—government employee. Required to dress up for work but not paid enough to look slick or stylish. Polite demeanor with just a hint of authority.

"You've got the right place," Luke said.

Keeping her out wasn't going to help Cindy in the long run.

"How can I help you?" Cindy said coolly.

"I'm from Social Services. I've had a report that you're living with a baby on this boat." Beverly Hicks looked pointedly at Adam, then at the stack of boxes.

Damn. The social worker had picked the worst possible time to show up—when the boat was redolent with a used Huggie. Luke grabbed the plastic bag that held the old diaper. "I'll take care of this." He'd seen a trash barrel on the dock and he exited the boat in search of it.

When he returned, Beverly was going through the same list of questions Luke had just asked Cindy—bathroom facilities, sleeping arrangements, heating and cooling. And she apparently didn't like the answers she was getting, judging from the frown and the decisive way she scribbled on a form attached to a clipboard.

Cindy wasn't exactly helping matters with her confrontational attitude, either.

"Ms. Hicks, does this baby look neglected or abused to you?"

Adam, at that moment, was bouncing on Cindy's knee, laughing as if this were the greatest entertainment in the world. Anyone could see he was happy, plump and healthy, dressed in clean clothes that fit him well.

"No, he looks very happy," Beverly agreed. "But I have to follow the guidelines," she added, not without sympathy. "Someone made a complaint about you."

"Who?" Cindy shot back. "Who complained?"

"I have to keep that information confidential. But I have to ascertain that certain criteria are being met. And clearly they aren't. The baby doesn't even have his own bed."

"He sleeps with me. Lots of parents let their little ones sleep in their bed."

"But the rules state the child has to have his own bed. And a place to bathe. And heat."

Oh, boy, Luke thought. He didn't like the sounds of this.

"This is only temporary," Luke put in. He extended his hand to the social worker. "I'm Deputy Sheriff Luke Rheems. I can vouch for Cindy—she's a really great mother."

Beverly shook his hand, silently appraising him. "I'm sure Ms. Lefler does the very best she can. Still, these arrangements aren't satisfactory. Adam is ambulatory. He could wake up, walk outside, fall off the boat and drown."

"That would never happen!" Cindy objected.

"Nevertheless, I'm afraid I'll have to take

temporary custody of Adam. We'll put him in foster care until you can make other living arrangements that meet the state's requirements."

Cindy looked horrified. She wrapped her arms around Adam. "You are not taking my baby. No. No way."

Beverly looked at Luke, pleading for understanding. "You're in law enforcement. You understand how these laws work, don't you?"

Unfortunately he did. But he agreed totally with Cindy. No way was Adam going into foster care. The mere thought of what could happen to a baby dropped into the hands of supposedly caring, qualified strangers made that instant coffee he'd drunk churn bitterly in his stomach.

"There must be some other way to deal with this," Cindy said, obviously struggling not to lose her cool completely.

"Well, if there's a qualified relative he could stay with," Beverly said. "What about the father? Is he in the picture?"

Cindy opened her mouth to answer, no doubt about to inform Beverly that the father was deceased. But Luke beat her to the punch.

"Actually, I'm Adam's father," he said. "Cindy and I were just discussing the possibility of Adam coming to live with me for a while until she can pull things together." He hadn't planned to tell such a whopper. It had just come out of his mouth, naturally as could be.

Cindy's jaw dropped, a denial ready, but Beverly smiled, obviously relieved. "Oh. Well, why didn't you say so? That's a different situation altogether. You two are on amicable terms, then?"

"Oh, yes," Luke answered quickly to keep Beverly's attention on him. Cindy was still gaping in shock, but so far she hadn't objected aloud.

"Do you have experience caring for a baby?" Beverly asked suspiciously, obviously doubting that this big, strapping lawman knew the difference between a diaper and a pacifier.

"Oh, yes, ma'am. I grew up in a foster home with lots of kids. I got real good at the diaper changing and bottle warming." As if to emphasize the point, he picked up Adam and cuddled him, knowing he would look perfectly natural and comfortable with the baby—and that Adam wouldn't object.

Beverly nodded. "What sort of child-care arrangements could you make while you're working?" she asked, taking notes now.

"My mother—well, she's my foster mother—

lives nearby. She's retired and I know she'd love taking care of Adam while I'm at work."

Beverly looked expectantly at Cindy, who had managed to school her face. "Is this arrangement satisfactory to you?"

"It's not ideal," she said. "But I'd rather that than foster care."

Beverly's eyes flickered with worry. "Do you have concerns about Deputy Rheems's ability to adequately care for Adam?"

Cindy shook her head. "No. He's very responsible. It's just—oh, never mind. It's fine."

Beverly smiled. "Very good, then. I'll get some information from you, then I'll check back in a day or two to make sure everything's A-OK."

"Thank you," Luke said, meaning it. Beverly took down some pertinent information about him—address, phone, work schedule, his foster mother's name and address. Then she turned her attention back to Cindy.

"Now, then. Is there anything I can do to help you? Do you need food? Diapers?"

"I'm not some welfare mother," Cindy said indignantly. "I've always paid my own way and I'll continue to do so."

Beverly seemed to frost over. "Excuse me, but I used to be a 'welfare mother,' as you call it. Everyone needs help now and then. Don't let your pride get in the way of common sense." She gave Adam a look of pity, tousled his downy hair, then saw herself out.

Luke and Cindy stared at each other in silence until the sound of Beverly's heels *thump-thumping* on the wooden dock receded into the distance.

"Are you out of your mind?" Cindy reached for Adam, who had started to fret.

"I should think you'd be thanking me. I kept that woman from taking Adam away, didn't I?"

"Yeah, with a huge lie! What's going to happen when she finds out the truth?"

"She won't find out."

"Of course she will! She'll go back to whoever made the complaint and tell them Adam's going to live with his father, and then she'll find out Adam's father is dead and all hell will break loose."

"Cindy, listen. Social workers have to adhere to privacy laws. If she tells the complainant anything, she'll simply say that the matter is taken care of. Don't worry."

"Don't worry?"

Adam's fussing got louder. Luke theorized the baby was responding more to the escalating tension than his hunger, but Cindy moved into the tiny galley and fished around in a box while jiggling Adam on one hip the way all mothers instinctively learned how to do. She produced a jar of baby cereal and a spoon.

"Don't worry—right." Her voice dripped with sarcasm. "That woman's going to be back, and she's going to expect to find Adam all cozy in your house, with his granny taking care of him."

"That's what she'll find, all right."

"Over my dead body. Just because you're a deputy sheriff doesn't mean you can take my kid away, so just get that out of your head."

Cindy pulled some orange juice from a cooler of melting ice and poured it into a Tommy Tippee cup. Adam eagerly reached for the cup, the juice magically silencing his fretting.

She wished Luke would just go away. He was too big for this little boat, his presence too overpowering. Even Beverly, a complete stranger, hadn't been immune to his sense of authority and the way his feet practically grew roots wherever he stood.

Cindy imagined Beverly hadn't been immune to Luke's sex appeal, either. What living, breathing woman could miss it? Though Beverly was at least ten years older than Luke, she'd batted her eyelashes at him like a teen-age girl with a crush.

He was impossible to ignore, though Cindy was trying her hardest.

"Maybe you missed what just happened," Luke said tightly, "but I'm trying my best to keep you and Adam together, not strip him away from you."

Cindy knew what he said was true. That was what Luke was all about—keeping families together. He was the best lawman Cotton-wood had ever seen. And though he was adept at solving crimes—the few there were in their little town—his main priority had always been helping kids, keeping them in school, keeping them off drugs. He volunteered a ton of hours at schools and churches and rec centers, orga-nizing after-school sports programs and home-work study groups.

"I'm sorry, Luke," she finally said. "This whole thing has just thrown me so off balance. I feel like a stray mother cat, hissing and claw-ing at anyone who comes near, even people trying to help."

She reclaimed her seat on the banquette, opened the jar of cereal and quietly began to feed Adam. Just recently he'd started grabbing the spoon on his own, trying to shove food into his own mouth. Today she didn't have the patience to clean up the results of such efforts, so they both held on to the spoon, managing to get most of the cereal into Adam rather than onto his shirt. He had bibs, but she didn't know where they were.

"You can't just ignore me and hope I'll go away," Luke continued. "You have to start dealing with the reality of your situation."

She sighed. "I know."

"I have an idea. There's a carriage-house apartment behind my house. It hasn't been used in years, but if memory serves, it has a bathroom and a kitchenette."

"No."

"Why not?"

"I can't afford rent." It was the first excuse that came to mind. What she really couldn't afford was to install herself so close to Luke. She was not immune to his appeal, despite all the years that had passed since they'd been lovers. Eight years of marriage, a baby plus her whirlwind affair—what else could she call it?—with Dex/Marvin, and she'd never once gone to sleep at night without at least a fleeting thought to her first love and what might have been if they'd wanted the same things out of life.

She didn't need that right now. Lord knew,

the last thing she could use in her life was a man, even if he was promising to help her out of a jam. Anyway, she didn't trust herself. She had the good judgment of a fungus, given her recent history.

"Did I say anything about rent? Come on, Cindy, the apartment's just sitting there. It's not much, and it'll have to be cleaned out and fixed up a bit, but it should make Social Services happy."

"I really wish you'd just leave me alone."

He stared at her, challenging, for a few seconds before dropping his gaze. "Yeah, I'll go. But you'll have to answer a few questions, first."

"Whatever."

"What should I tell Beverly Hicks when she comes calling tomorrow or the next day?"

"Tell her we changed our minds."

"Uh-huh. And when she comes back here? She will, you know. It's her job. You might think she's a nitpicking pain in the butt, but she cares about children or she wouldn't be in that line of work. And she's not going to sweep this under the rug. She'll be back, and next time she *will* take Adam. And if you won't give him up willingly, she will summon the law—me—to enforce her decision."

"Can she do that?" Cindy asked, feeling truly afraid for the first time.

He nodded grimly, his fists so tight he could feel his skin tightening over the knuckles. "It happens all the time. It happened to me, Cindy. And my mother never got me back."

Chapter Four

Luke didn't like bringing up his past. In all the time he'd known Cindy, even when they'd been in love and inseparable, he'd revealed little about his life before arriving in Cottonwood at age fourteen. Whenever she'd prompted him, he'd found a way to avoid giving her any real information.

As far as Cindy knew, Luke's life had begun at age fourteen when he'd landed with Polly Ferguson, the only foster parent who'd known how to handle him—the only one he'd ever stayed with longer than six months. He considered her his real mother now, and his foster brother,

Mike Baskin, was as close as any flesh-and-blood sibling.

So, no, he didn't like dredging up the more painful memories. But that had seemed the only way to shake Cindy out of her complacency. And it had. She'd agreed to move into his carriage house, though he could tell it had galled her to accept what she saw as charity. But better that than losing her son, even temporarily.

He'd needed to take care of some sheriffing business, but he returned to the marina later that afternoon with a horse trailer. He and Cindy loaded up her meager belongings in about five minutes.

"Adam will need a crib," she said, breaking a long silence. "Do you think that awful Ed LaRue will let me get the old one from my—from his house?"

"He put all your furniture out in the street," Luke said. "I drove by your place earlier, just to check on things."

"I guess I don't blame him. He was probably madder than a cornered javelina hog to find all that junk I left behind." She actually grinned at the thought. "I probably should have put it in storage or something," she admitted. "It was just garage-sale stuff, nothing good, but I might need it."

"Let's go see what's there." Luke was encouraged to hear Cindy actually thinking ahead more than ten minutes. She'd always been a girl with plans—big plans. To see her in survival mode, refusing to think about tomorrow, much less next month or next year, was painful.

Luke was relieved to see Cindy's furniture still lined up at the edge of her yard—Ed's yard—with a big sign stuck to her dining room table that said Free Stuff.

"I don't see the crib," Cindy said. "Probably somebody took it already. And my bed isn't here, either. Damn, what was I thinking?"

"Nobody really expected you to be thinking clearly after what happened to you. It's okay. I bet Polly has an extra crib. Which of this stuff do you want?"

"All of it," she said decisively, rolling up the sleeves of her sweatshirt. "Whatever I can't use, I'll sell."

"That's the spirit." It was wonderful to hear that determination in her voice and see a sparkle in her eye. They loaded up a table and chairs, some bookshelves, a sofa, nightstands, a couple of lamps and pictures and a TV cabinet.

"I guess the TV and VCR are gone," she said wistfully as they pushed and shoved the furniture so it would all fit. "What was I thinking?"

"Stop questioning yourself so much, honey." The endearment slipped out, and Luke resisted slapping his hand over his mouth. Her eyes flashed at him, but that was all. "Cut yourself some slack, okay? Focus on the future."

"Yeah, the future," she murmured.

She was going to have to make some major readjustments in her thinking. Nowhere in her wildest imaginings had she pictured herself broke and without a source of income. She'd always worked—always. And though she'd never been exactly wealthy, she'd never wanted for anything basic, even those years she'd lived in a truck. Of course, she hadn't had a baby in tow.

"So, do you have any plans?" Luke asked, forcing the question to sound casual.

"I haven't thought much about it," she admitted as he closed the tailgate on the trailer. They got back into his Blazer. Adam was snoozing in his car seat in back, and not even the slam of the tailgate had awakened him.

He would be such a great traveling companion, she thought for the umpteenth time. And dammit, she wasn't giving up on the idea of traveling with him. She just had to figure out how. "I guess I'll have to get a job."

"In a restaurant?"

"Maybe, though I can't think of any place around here that's looking for help."

"What else are you qualified to do?"

"Drive. But I can't see me driving without Jim. And without my own rig…" She stopped there, thinking about Jim's truck, how he'd fixed it up so fine and painted his own logo on the sides. He'd had dreams of owning his own fleet of trucks. It would have happened, too. He'd have made it happen.

She swallowed back tears. Oh, God, she couldn't start crying again. When she started, she had a hard time stopping. And she didn't want Luke to see her weeping. He must already think she was a candidate for a straitjacket.

"Trucking isn't a safe job for a woman alone, much less with a child," Luke commented as he pulled his Blazer into the street, the trailer rattling behind them.

"No," she agreed, grateful he'd eased over the awkward moment. If he'd offered sympathy, she'd have lost it.

"So the restaurant industry is your best bet. But you should be more ambitious. You've got management experience now—managing a staff, keeping the books…"

"Who in their right mind would trust me with money?" She sighed. "Anyway, that sort of job would require me to put together a résumé and go through interviews. I'd rather just walk in someplace, put on an apron and wait tables." She knew she sounded pathetically unambitious.

Luke didn't say anything else about her future. He was probably frustrated with her attitude, and she couldn't blame him. She just wasn't herself.

He pulled in the driveway of his house—a big, old, prairie-style frame home with a front porch that spanned its entire width.

"This house is bigger than I remembered," she said idly. "I thought you'd have filled it full of kids by now."

"What woman would have me?" he quipped, but his smile seemed slightly forced. He pulled all the way around to the back, where there was a detached garage—three narrow stalls with a second story above them. "I haven't been inside the carriage house in a long time. Last time I checked, it was okay, though."

And what if it isn't now? Cindy wondered.

They parked and climbed out. Adam was awake now, looking around curiously. Odd that he'd slept through the slamming trailer door, but pulling quietly into a driveway had awakened him. Cindy had long suspected he was extremely sensitive to her moods. Now he sensed her anxiety about her new temporary home.

The baby held his arms toward Cindy. "Ma-ma-ma-ma."

She grinned. "Luke, did you hear that? He said *mama.*"

"Is that the first time?" Luke seemed to share her wonder. He came around to her side of the car and peered in at Adam when she opened the back door.

"He's been vocalizing for a while now, and sometimes it's hard to tell whether he's actually saying something or just babbling." She unbuckled the various straps on the car seat and extracted Adam. "But that was pretty clear. He was looking at me and reaching for me and saying *mama.*" She hugged her son. "You're such a smart boy, aren't you, Adam." Those pesky tears returned to her eyes, but these weren't tears of despair. She was suddenly awash in sentimentality. And there was Luke, standing too close, almost touching, and she felt as if she ought to be resentful toward him due to the simple fact that he wasn't Jim, he *wasn't* Adam's father, and a boy's father should be there when he speaks his first words.

But resentment was only a tiny part of what

she felt. It was such a bittersweet moment, and mostly she was just glad that she'd been able to share it with someone. She'd borne so much all alone since Jim's death. Adam had only been two months old. Jim had missed his first steps, his first tooth, the ear infection that had sent her flying to a Tyler hospital in a dead panic. Then her mother's unexpected death.

No wonder she'd turned to Dex so easily. Finally there had been someone to lean on, someone to confide in and share the burden as well as the joys. She must have been an incredibly easy target.

All at once, she couldn't keep the tears at bay and she sobbed.

"Cindy?"

She couldn't bear the concern in Luke's voice. She wanted to hit him. She wanted to put her arms around him and never let go. But then she'd be doing it again, falling all over the first man to show an interest in her, the first man to act as if he cared.

With Dex, all he'd really cared about was getting into her bed and her bank accounts. She knew Luke didn't want to steal her money. But what did he want, really? And was she in any position to figure it out?

"I'm s-sorry." She wiped her eyes, getting

the tears under control before they could turn into a full-fledged crying jag. "Sometimes it just h-hits me."

Thankfully Luke didn't make a big deal of it. He grabbed a couple of tissues from a travel box he kept in his glove compartment and handed them to her. Then he busied himself with finding the key to the carriage house while she wiped her eyes and blew her nose while juggling Adam from hip to hip.

"Okay," she said, taking a deep breath. "Let's see this apartment."

She walked up the stairs ahead of him, then stood aside on the landing so she could unlock the door, which led directly into the tiny kitchenette. They both entered, then recoiled from a nasty smell.

"Did something die in here?" Cindy asked, only half kidding.

"It's been closed up for a long time," Luke said. "Probably just needs a good cleaning and airing out."

Cindy didn't particularly look forward to that. She'd spent the last two days scrubbing down the boat to make it habitable. And it hadn't smelled nearly this bad.

She moved on into the living room holding Adam tightly. She didn't dare set him down in this nasty place. Luke, directly behind her, flipped on a light. Three huge, gray creatures jumped and hissed, then scuttled for cover beneath a reprobate sofa.

Cindy screamed and nearly ran over Luke as she tried to get as far away as possible from the critters. Adam started crying.

"Oh, my God," she said from the relative safety of the kitchen. "What were those things?"

"Possums," Luke said grimly. "Guess the carriage house wasn't uninhabited, after all." He laughed. "Those were some big ones, too. I think we scared them more than they scared us."

"Speak for yourself. I'll be waiting outside."

She couldn't get down the stairs fast enough. As she waited by the Blazer, calming Adam down, her terror receded. In its place a slow anger started to burn. She had a trailer full of stuff and nowhere to put it. She put Adam down on a small patch of grass. He liked grass, always had. He dropped to his hands and knees and crawled slowly across it, stopping every second or so to pat the soft green blades with the palms of his hands, investigating the texture. He pressed his face into it.

Luke came down the stairs a couple of minutes later. "Well, I figured out how the possums got in. There's a broken window in the bedroom. Also, there's a pretty bad leak in the roof. That's going to have to be fixed, and the carpeting pulled out."

"So, in short, it's not livable."

"I'm afraid not."

"And you're just figuring this out now?" Whatever warmth she'd felt for him a few minutes earlier had dissipated like a morning fog.

"I guess I should have checked it out before—"

"Yeah, no kidding! The boat might not have been ideal, but at least it didn't have disgusting creatures nesting in the furniture." Other than a few spiders, but she'd dislodged them in short order.

"I'll fix the damned place. You can bunk in my spare bedroom until I get the carriage house fixed up. Shouldn't be more than a few days."

"Oh, you'd like that, wouldn't you?"

Luke looked surprised by her outburst.

"You knew all along the carriage house wasn't livable," she went on. "You just used that as an excuse to get us under your roof so you could…trap us."

"Trap you?" he said incredulously.

"You think we'll get so comfy in your big

house that we won't want to leave. And that will prove you're right."

"Right about what?"

"About how children should be raised. All along you've thought I was a bad mother for wanting to travel with Adam, take him away from Cottonwood. You've wanted to settle down with this white-picket-fence stuff since we were eighteen. Now you've got us—no place to go, no choice but to move in with you."

Suddenly a horrible thought occurred to her. "I'm so stupid. It was you who made the complaint to Social Services, wasn't it? And how convenient, that you just happened to be there when the social worker came to investigate."

Luke's face turned ruddy with anger. He folded his arms, as if to stop himself from throttling her. "How could you think I would do something like that?" he exploded. "And I have no hidden agenda here except to help you keep Adam. I'm sorry about the carriage house. If you don't want to stay with me, fine. I'll take you back to the boat and you can sink with it."

Adam had pushed himself to his feet and was making tracks, heading for a row of bushes. Cindy caught him before he could disappear into the shrubs and never be seen again, gently swiveling him around. He toddled off in the opposite direction, seemingly unaware his path had been diverted.

What was she doing, attacking the only person in any position to help her? Beverly Hicks had been right—her damnable pride would defeat her if she let it.

She put a hand to her forehead. "God, I'm sorry, Luke. All right, I'll move into your spare bedroom. But only temporarily, until I'm back on my feet."

"I never intended for it to be a permanent situation." His brief spate of temper dissipated immediately. "Come on, I'll show you the room. I converted the attic into a suite. You'll be on a completely different floor than me."

The suite wasn't just nice, it was dollhouse pretty, with shiny oak floors and pale yellow walls with white trim. There was one small bedroom, a larger, central room and a tiny, yellow-tiled bathroom tucked under the eaves.

"This is beautiful," she said grudgingly. And in a flash, she realized what Luke had been thinking when he'd renovated his attic. He'd intended this area for a child, maybe two. The central room was a playroom. Her heart lurched slightly at the thought of Luke's hopes for a family still unfulfilled after all these years.

Then she gave herself a mental slap. He

was only twenty-eight. He had lots and lots of time to find that settling-down girl he'd always wanted. And it wasn't as if he *had* to be alone. With his sexy good looks, he could have women lining up to marry him if he really tried.

She'd spent a lot of years feeling guilty because she hadn't been the one. She wasn't going to feel guilty about that anymore. She had enough to worry about.

Luke hadn't realized how anxious he was about Cindy's plans until she finally agreed to stay in his spare room. As soon as she said okay, his muscles relaxed and the tightness in his chest eased. They were going to be fine. Cindy and Adam had a safe haven, and there was no way Beverly Hicks would object to Adam's housing.

He called his brother, Mike, who lived only about ten minutes away, and together they moved Cindy's furniture into the attic suite while Cindy fed Adam. The pieces that didn't fit, they stored in the garage.

Cindy didn't take an active role in the arrangement of her new space. When Mike asked her where the table and chairs should go, she shrugged. "Any place it'll fit, I guess." She busied herself with more practical things, such as putting sheets on the twin bed and on the crib, which Polly had brought over.

Polly hadn't stayed—she had five kids, her current batch of foster children, to fix dinner for. But she'd paused long enough to fuss over Adam and give Cindy a warm hug, drawing the younger woman against her ample bosom and patting her on the back with her large, bony, work-roughened hands.

No one could fail to feel better after a hug from Polly. Luke remembered the first time he'd felt it himself. Fourteen years old, kicked out of his last three foster homes, belligerent and secretly terrified. And there was big, soft Polly, with her unapologetically gray hair and her ever-present apron. She'd smelled like fresh-baked cookies. And though Luke had just cursed at her and told her to get the hell away from him, she'd forcibly wrapped her arms around him and whispered to him, "It's all going to be different from now on."

People had told him that before, but he'd never really believed it until Polly said it, her words so confident, no question in her voice or in her mind.

Luke had walked her out to her car. "Thanks, Polly. I knew you'd come through."

"Oh, it's nothing." She'd waved away his

gratitude. "Luke, are you sure you know what you're doing? I mean, I'll always have a soft spot for Cindy. But she broke your heart last time you gave her a chance."

"I'm not involved with her," Luke had said quickly. "I'm just helping her out."

Polly had raised her eyebrows in question. "That so? You don't have some ulterior motive? Like proving how good a husband and provider you could be?"

"Aw, Polly, come on." But that was exactly what Cindy had accused him of not two hours earlier.

"Well, just be careful. Call if you need anything. You know I'd be pleased to babysit little Adam anytime."

Polly had driven off in her old rattletrap station wagon, and Luke had just stood in the driveway, staring down the street at nothing in particular, wondering if Cindy's and Polly's suspicions about him weren't just a little bit true.

He really hadn't realized how bad a condition the carriage house was in. And he certainly hadn't been the one to call Social Services and report Cindy as a bad mother—he wasn't that overtly devious. But maybe there was some part of him that cheered at the idea of Cindy and Adam living under his roof, the surrogate family he'd never had. Maybe in the back of his mind he *did* believe he could convince Cindy that she'd made a mistake not marrying him in the first place.

It had been a year since Jim's death. And hadn't Luke planned to reignite his and Cindy's passion once that year had passed? Never mind that Marvin Carter had fouled up his plans for a while. That scumbag was gone now. If Luke lost his chance again, if some other opportunistic jerk swooped in and plucked up Cindy now, it wouldn't be because Luke was sitting on his thumbs.

At the very least, he was obligated to protect her from con men and scam artists while she was in this vulnerable state. And what better way to protect her than to have her living under his roof? What unscrupulous guy would dare approach her while she was living with a deputy sheriff?

All these alien thoughts were a little frightening for Luke, who'd never thought of himself as devious. But the plan that was formulating now was definitely less than aboveboard. All was fair in love and war—right?

Later that evening, Cindy was almost out of diapers for Adam. She checked her wallet—

three dollars and twenty-eight cents. She had some cloth ones and rubber pants she could use in a pinch, but she'd gotten spoiled by the disposables, which honestly were as good as the TV commercials made them out to be. All at once, she was overwhelmed with unreasonable anger, and she finally knew who to aim it at. Not herself, for being naive. Certainly not Luke, whose only sin was trying to help. And not Jim or her mother, for dying and leaving her alone. The person who deserved her anger was Marvin Carter. Because of him, Adam would probably get diaper rash.

And it could have been worse. Her baby could have been taken away from her, given to strangers. And all because Marvin Carter was greedy and got a kick out of pulling the wool over the eyes of vulnerable women and sucking them dry.

No one messed with her kid and got away with it. Frankly, she wondered why it had taken her this long to work up a good head of steam.

No more pitiful Cindy. It was time she fought back. She was going to nail Marvin Carter's butt to the wall and get her money back. That money was Jim's final gift to her, his legacy to Adam.

She went to her purse and pulled out the card

Sonya had given her, with the cell phone number. She hoped those two women were still in town. She intended to join forces with them and track Marvin Carter, then run him down like the rabid dog he was.

Hell hath no fury like a woman scorned, the saying went. Well, how about *three* women scorned? Marvin Carter probably hadn't *dreamed* of the fury he was going to have to deal with.

Chapter Five

That first night under Luke's roof, Cindy slept better than she had in a week. His house was much quieter than hers, she realized. Quieter neighborhood and better insulated. No passing cars or barking dogs woke her up.

When Adam's happy morning babble awakened her at seven-thirty, she felt better than she had since that awful day almost two weeks ago. She felt full of energy and purpose.

Cindy bathed herself and Adam, then dressed with care in khaki slacks and a blue silk T-shirt. She was going to have to apply for jobs today. She pulled her hair up in a clip at the base of her neck, making sure all stray ends were tucked in, then filed her fingernails and applied lotion. No one wanted to hire a waitress with messy hair or ugly hands.

But first things first. She'd arranged to meet with Sonya and Brenna at the Kountry Kozy B and B at nine, and they were going to come up with a plan for nailing Marvin's hide to the wall.

Downstairs, Luke's house was dark and quiet, and Cindy felt a stab of disappointment. He'd cooked dinner for her last night. Just hamburgers, but she'd shamelessly enjoyed letting him wait on her. It had been so long since anyone had taken care of her. It was amazing how quickly she could get used to it, too. She was actually disappointed that he wasn't here at her beck and call, frying eggs for her.

She shook her head and cautioned herself not to get too used to this. She was going to get her money back. And then she was going to travel with Adam. Maybe she wouldn't go first-class all the way, as she and the fictional Dex had planned, but with three-quarters of a million dollars, she could see a lot. Provided Marvin hadn't already spent it all.

She did find a note from Luke: "Cindy, Make yourself at home. Back around four. Polly will babysit for Adam anytime. Luke."

And he'd left her a key.

She decided to take Polly up on her offer. Adam would just be a distraction during her meeting with her fellow scam victims. And it wouldn't look good taking him with her to apply for jobs.

As she pulled up in front of Polly's huge, two-story house, all sorts of unexpected feelings hit her. She'd spent a lot of time here during high school, when she and Luke had been together every minute they could manage. Her memories of Polly Ferguson's home were warm ones—always a pack of kids running around, screaming and laughing and fighting, and Polly always in the kitchen, delivering equal shares of love and discipline. The house had smelled of good food—beef stew or cinnamon rolls, spaghetti sauce, chocolate cake. And it was always chaotic and messy but never dirty. Polly had encouraged her foster kids to take pride in the place they called home, even if it was temporary.

And they all lived to please her. They arrived here wounded little birds with broken wings, surly, some of them downright delinquents. And even those who stayed only a short time returned to their regular homes in better shape than when they'd left.

As Cindy climbed the front steps of the old house, she could already smell bread baking. Polly answered the bell, her face wreathed with a warm smile, looking the same as always. Oh, maybe her hair was a little more gray, her face a bit more wrinkled, but she hadn't slowed down one iota.

"Oh, Cindy, I'm so glad you took my offer to heart. Come in, come in. Hi, Adam. How are you today?"

Adam grinned and held his arms out to Polly as if she were a favorite grandmother.

"Who's in your brood these days?" Cindy asked.

Polly propped Adam on one hip, and they wandered into the kitchen. Ten years seemed to melt away. "Well, I've got a set of twins, Amber and Ashley. They're twelve, in school of course. And I've still got Bobby. He's eighteen now and in vo-tech. I 'spect he'll be going out on his own pretty soon. Then there are two little ones, four and five, Michelle and Ben. They're gonna go crazy over you," she said to Adam, as if he could understand. Then to Cindy she said, "You want some tea?"

"I really need to get moving." She set Adam's diaper bag on the floor. "I'm almost out of diapers," she admitted.

Polly waved away her concern. "I've always got diapers. You run along now. I'll keep Adam as long as you need me to."

"Oh, Polly, you're so good. I should think you would kick me right out the door after... well, after what I did."

"All you did was follow your own heart, girl. No sin in that. Anyway, that's ancient history."

Cindy gave Polly a hug, said goodbye to Adam—who was so wound up in Polly he hardly noticed his mother's departure—and set out for the Kountry Kozy B and B on the town square.

Parking was always at a premium on the square. Cindy had never had to worry about it before—she'd always parked in her reserved spot behind the Miracle Café. But she no longer had that option. She drove around the square twice before she found a spot, fed quarters into the meter, then set out on foot for the other side.

On the way, she was forced to pass the café. She'd tried not to look at it as she'd driven past, but on foot she could hardly miss it. The Miracle Café awning was gone, as was her neon light that had flickered in the front window for close to fifty years. Now there was an orange banner advertising Grand Opening! and a temporary, hand-painted sign over the front door: Ed's Enchilada Emporium.

Cindy had never imagined she could feel nostalgic for the café. Her whole life she'd wanted nothing more than to get away from it. And during those eight years she'd been away, she'd never missed it. But maybe because she'd known it would always be there, waiting for her, whenever she felt a need to return.

Now it was gone forever, nothing but a memory. She didn't even have any pictures of it. Not being the nostalgic type, she'd kept only a few family photographs so she could show Adam his ancestors. The rest she'd tossed when she'd liquidated her mom's estate.

She hurried past the café, refusing to even peek in the window to see what Ed LaRue had done to the decor.

The Kountry Kozy B and B was housed in an old Victorian painted lady, now a raucous pink with purple trim. The house had been an abandoned wreck at one time during Cindy's childhood, slated for demolition, but a nice couple from Dallas had saved it at the last minute, then had sunk a fortune into renovating it. Other homes and businesses on the square had followed the B and B's lead, and soon they'd had tearooms and antique malls. Even the insurance agency and the Tri-County Realty office had decorative awnings and brightly painted molding, though the buildings themselves were newer.

She climbed the steps and let herself in. "Hello?"

"We're in the parlor," a female voice called. Cindy followed the sound of it and found Sonya and Brenna perched on the delicate camelback sofa.

And Luke standing near the front window, his large frame haloed by the morning light filtering through gauze curtains. What was he doing here? She couldn't suppress the rush of pleasure she felt at seeing him, as if it had been weeks instead of only a few hours. How had he become so central to her existence in such a short time? And was he doing it on purpose?

"We asked Deputy Rheems to sit in on our discussion," Sonya explained. "Since some of Marvin's crimes occurred in his jurisdiction, he has agreed to be our law-enforcement liaison."

Brenna rolled her eyes and made a soft huffing sound, indicating pretty clearly what she thought of law enforcement.

Cindy nodded, though she wished she could

just drop through a crack in the floor. It was difficult enough admitting how stupid she'd been to these other women, who she presumed had been just as dumb. But with Luke as a witness, she wasn't sure she could go through with it. Sonya and Brenna would go away, but Luke she would see every day. And every time she saw him, she would have to relive this humiliation.

Then she thought about Adam and his future, his college fund, money for braces or glasses if he needed them, and she sharpened her resolve. So what if she was embarrassed? She was going to get her money back.

Cindy pulled a wingback chair closer to the coffee table. Fran Bressler, the Kountry Kozy's owner, had laid out some hot tea and her special home-baked fig bars. Because Cindy had skipped breakfast—she hadn't felt right rummaging through Luke's fridge—she grabbed one of the soft cookies and ate it. Once she had her sugar fix, she was ready.

"I do have some information that might help," she said as she opened a large manila envelope and dumped the contents onto the table. She might have been in a stupor after Marvin had left her high and dry, but some part of her had remained sane enough to gather up this stuff and protect it.

Sonya and Brenna both reached for the photographs, three very clear candids taken at the café. "He grew a beard," Sonya said excitedly.

"And cut his hair," Brenna added. "When he was posing as an art dealer, his hair was down to his shoulders and he had an earring. How did you get these pictures? Marvin's normally very camera shy."

"One of my customers at the diner is the photographer for the *Cottonwood Conversation*," said Cindy. "I had him sneak those pictures for me. Dex—I mean, Marvin—made it very clear he did not like cameras. But I wanted some—" She stopped and looked at Luke, feeling her face heat up.

"Something to remind you of him when he was gone," Sonya finished for her. "I know what you mean. Well, these are great."

"A police artist can alter them to show what he might look like clean-shaven," Luke added. "Or with glasses."

"Yeah, but who do we give the pictures to?" Brenna asked. "The stupid FBI isn't interested in our help."

"I have some contacts," Luke said. "I'll see

if I can't get someone interested on a national level. This guy is clearly a repeat offender. I'm willing to bet you three aren't the first women he's victimized."

"I just wish we knew where he went from here."

"I might be able to help with that, too," Cindy said, sifting through the other papers she'd brought. "This is a recent cell phone bill, showing exactly when he called from out of town. I bet the phone company could pinpoint where he actually was."

"Maybe with his newest conquest," Sonya said glumly. "I wish we could stop him *before* he does this to someone else."

"If you'd found me a few days earlier," Cindy pointed out, "you'd have had him. How did you find me, anyway?"

"I followed him," Brenna said. "Several weeks ago, I started to suspect he was cheating on me. I followed him as far as Woodson, but I ran out of gas. We've been checking all the towns from Woodson."

Cindy was seething. "You mean he was still seeing you while he was—oh, that *rat!* I never even suspected…"

"Your eyes were still glazed over with love,"

said Sonya. "I imagine we were all like that at first. I was. I saw only what I wanted to see."

"I didn't love him," Cindy murmured. The others chose to let her comment pass.

"What else have you got in that stack of stuff?" Brenna asked, glossing over the awkward moment.

"I've got copies of the power-of-attorney documents I signed. They've got the name of a Houston law firm on them. Also, I ran by the bank and got copies of the documents he signed when he stole all my money. He's got a very distinctive signature."

"We can get the original from the bank," Luke said, "and check it for fingerprints."

"Great idea!" said Sonya enthusiastically. "We've never managed to get prints on him. We're not even a hundred percent sure Marvin Carter is his real name. It might be another alias."

"How many did he have?" Cindy asked, getting more and more intrigued and revolted by the depth of this man's deceit.

"We think there must have been at least half a dozen before us," Sonya said, "given his age and how good he is at the game."

"His type usually starts small," Luke added, "ripping off relatives and girlfriends. They start with crimes of convenience. Someone leaves a checkbook lying around or drops a Social Security number. Then it starts to be deliberate. Then, when he's alienated everyone he knows and he's gotten away with it, he gets bolder. He starts targeting women who have money."

"I'm just curious," Cindy said, "but how did he suck you girls in?"

"With me, he pretended to be an art agent," Brenna said. "I'm a jewelry designer, and like most artists, I'm a little desperate to find fame. That was the button he pushed. Along with the romance one, of course. Then he made off with my money-market fund and all of my inventory, including some of my grandmother's jewelry."

"I was really easy," Sonya admitted shamefacedly. "I was desperate for someone who would appreciate *me,* not my bank account. But every guy I ever liked was a fortune hunter—or so my mother believed. She chased off every man who so much as looked my way. Except Marvin. Old money, you know. He had her completely buffaloed. Since I had no money of my own, he went for my credit cards and jewelry, even some paintings."

Sonya had pictures of her own—insurance

photographs of her jewelry collection, enough gold and diamonds to sink the Titanic.

Cindy gasped when she recognized one particular piece, a yellow diamond pendant surrounded by more diamonds. "He gave this one to me as a gift," she said. "But one of the stones was loose. He said he was sending it for repair."

"What a scum," Brenna grumbled. "Did he give you any silver jewelry?"

Cindy shook her head. "I have just one more clue. I found these under the passenger seat of the Porsche. I had dropped some change and went looking for it." She pointed to a book of matches from a restaurant called Kakki's Bon-ton Maison in Smoky Bayou, Louisiana.

Everyone leaned over the table to look at the matches, including Luke. He was close enough that Cindy could smell his aftershave and see the tiny red dot on his chin where he'd nicked himself shaving.

All of a sudden she was eighteen again, wanting to throw her arms around him, bury her face against his chest, but unable to because they always had an audience. Between the long hours they'd both worked, school, Cindy's pro-tective parents and a pack of kids from Polly's house that followed them around like puppies, it had taken unbelievable planning and sneakiness for them to be alone long enough to make out, much less make love.

But they'd managed it. More than a couple of times.

Cindy shook herself. No, no, no. She wasn't going to throw herself at any man just because she was unhappy with her current state of affairs. She'd always looked for a man to rescue her, to remove her from Cottonwood and take her on adventures. She'd been lucky with Jim, that he'd been such a good man, someone she could admire and love.

But just look at the mistake she'd made with Dex.

This time she wasn't going to depend on a man to fix her life. She was going to get her money back and then live her life on her terms. She did not want or need a man in the picture— especially not Luke, who was so rooted in Cottonwood she was surprised he could lift his feet to walk.

"I'll bet that's where his newest conquest is," Brenna said excitedly. "Smoky Bayou, Louisiana."

"Since that real-estate-developer line worked

so well on Cindy," Sonya said, "he might be using it again. Maybe he's decided big cities like Houston and Dallas are too risky, and small towns where people are more, um, less, um—"

"More ignorant?" Cindy provided. "Less sophisticated?"

"That's not what I meant at all," Sonya said, drawing herself up frostily. "Less connected to large law-enforcement agencies. That's what I meant."

Cindy didn't think so. Then again, both of these women were obviously upper-class, neither ignorant nor unsophisticated, yet that hadn't protected either of them from Marvin.

"I think we should go to this little Smoky Bayou and look for him," Brenna declared.

"He might have just stopped at this restaurant on the way to or from somewhere else," Luke pointed out.

"Maybe, but I don't think so," Cindy said. "It looks like a fancy restaurant. The kind of place you go to impress a woman."

Sonya found a road atlas tucked in one of the B and B's bookcases. All four of them huddled over the map of Louisiana, searching for Smoky Bayou. Luke was so close to Cindy now, his shoulder touched hers.

She shot him an accusing look, positive he was crowding her on purpose, but he was focused on the map.

"There it is." Sonya pointed with one perfectly polished acrylic nail. "And it doesn't look like it's on the way to or from *anywhere*. Do you think he just throws a dart at a map?"

"He could find lonely women in Internet chat rooms," said Brenna.

"I've never even been on the Internet," Cindy argued.

"He might have any number of strategies for locating his victims," Luke said. "I'll contact law enforcement in this Smoky Bayou, see if I can find anything out."

"I think we should go there," Brenna said.

"Me, too," said Sonya. "We've come this far. What about you, Cindy?"

"I'd love to. But I'm flat broke."

"Oh, don't worry about that," Sonya said. "I've still got one credit card Marvin didn't know about. And my mother pays the bill." She laughed—a trifle bitterly, Cindy thought.

She had to admit the idea of getting out of town appealed to her. And though she had little in common with either of these women, they did share the bond of being victims. By virtue of that alone, she was starting to like them, feel comfortable with them, even if they did think she was a small-town hick.

"All right, then, I'm in," she said impulsively. "After all, I've got almost three-quarters of a million dollars on the line."

The room went very, very still.

"What? What did I say?"

"Three-quarters of a million dollars?" Luke repeated. "What were you doing with that much money?"

"That's more than what he took from us—combined," Brenna said.

Cindy addressed Luke with her answer. "Not that it's any of your business, but my parents had squirreled away quite a bit of money. The Miracle Café was a cash cow. And Jim had a humongous life-insurance policy."

"With that much money, I guess I don't blame you for wanting to sell the café and enjoy life," Luke said softly, staring out the window.

"And that's just what I'm going to do, too, when I get my money back."

"That's the spirit," Sonya said. "How quick can you get packed up?"

As always, the idea of packing a bag and climbing into a car headed for parts unknown filled her with an indescribable thrill. "Like, ten minutes?"

Luke cleared his throat. "Um, Cindy, aren't you forgetting something?"

"I don't—oh." She was such an idiot. Adam. She couldn't ride off into the sunset and leave Adam. Good Lord, how could she have forgotten her own son, even for a minute?

"What's the problem?" Brenna asked.

"I have a little boy," she said. "Although he's no trouble, this might not be the best trip to bring along a baby."

"We didn't realize you had a kid," Brenna said. "I suppose Marvin played the part of the devoted would-be dad."

"You suppose right," Cindy said, recalling how her phony fiancé had spent endless hours entertaining Adam, putting him on his shoulders, rocking him to sleep, feeding him, even changing his diaper. "And Adam adored him."

"Adam adores everyone," Luke reminded her.

"Bring the tyke along," Brenna said. "We won't let anything happen to him."

Cindy glanced at Luke. His face looked like a thunderstorm, indicating exactly how he felt about the idea of her dragging Adam on a fugitive hunt.

"No, I really can't," she finally said. If Beverly Hicks came back and found her and Adam gone, she would probably send the National Guard after her. "I need to look for a job. I'm sort of homeless."

Brenna shook her head. "Man, that sucks."

They said their goodbyes. Brenna and Sonya promised to stay in touch with Luke and report their progress, while Luke said he would work on the fingerprints, the phone bill, the police-artist sketches and the Dallas law firm.

"I wish I could do something," Cindy said as Luke casually walked with her toward her car as if he were merely headed in the same direction by coincidence.

"Sooner or later this guy will get caught, Cindy," he said. "He's getting bolder. I had no idea he'd stolen so much from you. And if he went across the state line, that's definitely FBI territory."

"Sonya and Cindy said they already went to the FBI."

"Yeah, well, they won't brush me aside so easily."

She again looked the other way as they passed Ed's Enchilada Emporium, but she couldn't avoid the nauseating smell emanat-

ing from the place—burned corn, peppers, on-
ions and another odor she couldn't quite put
her finger on. "He's not doing much business."

"I'm not surprised if the inside smells as bad
as the outside." Unable to resist temptation, she
joined Luke at the window. "Oh, my gosh, the
décor alone would give me indigestion." The
walls had been painted tomato-red and mustard-
yellow. Neon-colored serapes and gaudy, gold-
embroidered sombreros were hung and draped
all over the place. On one wall was a huge velvet
painting of a bullfight. The light fixtures had
been replaced with chandeliers in the shape of
giant red peppers.

A part of her despised Ed LaRue and was
glad his grand opening was a flop. But then
she felt guilty. Maybe this was Ed's dream of a
lifetime. He was a victim of Marvin's as much
as she was. He might not even know why she'd
been so hostile and uncooperative, although
surely someone had told him by now.

"It's a shame, isn't it?"

Cindy looked over her shoulder to see Allison Hardison, Cottonwood's dentist.

"There ought to be a law against tasteless
decorating," she added. "I don't know a single
person who will set foot in the place. Aside from

the fact that it would feel disloyal to you and your family, the smell alone keeps me away."

"Maybe we should give poor Ed a chance," Cindy found herself saying. "It's not his fault, what happened to me. He just wound up in the middle of it."

Allison shivered delicately. "He's an obnoxious, hateful man, and his wife's even worse. She threw a fit in my waiting room yesterday because she came in with a toothache and no appointment and thought I should drop everything. I was in the middle of a root canal. What was I supposed to do? Even if the LaRues hadn't stolen the Miracle Café, they've alienated half the people in town already. I wouldn't give them a dime's worth of my business."

Cindy grinned. She knew it was evil, but she couldn't help being tickled by Allison's loyalty to her.

"Mark my words," Allison continued, "he'll be out of business in a month and hightailing it home to whatever rock he crawled out from under." She nodded, punctuating her prediction, then continued down the sidewalk.

"I think she's right," Luke said. "Maybe when that happens you can buy it back."

"Buy it back? You must be crazy. I've wanted to be free of that place ever since I moved back here. Even if I recover some or all of my money, the last thing I would do is reopen the café. I'm out of here, Luke, one way or another. Get used to the idea."

Chapter Six

Luke felt sad at Cindy's pronouncement. Some people searched for a home, a place to belong, their whole lives. Here Cindy had a place where she was loved and admired, where just about anyone would stick his neck out to help her. And all she could talk about was leaving it.

"I just don't get you," he said as they continued down the sidewalk toward their cars. "We're your friends. You heard Allison. Everyone in this town is so loyal to you, they won't set foot in the Enchilada Emporium."

"If the food was any good, they'd be here. It's easy to be loyal when you don't have to sacrifice anything."

"You really believe that?"

She felt a twinge of guilt at dismissing the townspeople's silent support. "Oh, I don't know what I believe. I just know that I don't want to be stuck here doing the same old thing as always. Some people find a routine to be comfortable, but to me it's a rut."

"Just because you live in a small town doesn't mean every day has to be exactly the same."

"It does if you own a café. Luke, I make biscuits in my sleep."

"So forget the café. You could do anything."

"Exactly my point. I'm getting my money back and then I'm going to travel." They'd reached Cindy's car. "We're just very different, you and I," she concluded.

"That didn't used to stop us," Luke said, his voice low and sexy. "I like to think of us as complementary. You add spice to my dull life. I provide the grounding and stability you need. It used to work pretty well."

"We were just kids," she protested.

He moved closer, backing her against the car. "We were happy kids. We had so much fun."

"We had so much sex, you mean."

A slow grin came to his face as he closed his eyes, apparently recalling their naughty past. "Oh, yeah." His eyes popped back open.

"But we had other kinds of fun, too, and you know it."

She couldn't deny it. Sure, they'd enjoyed discovering each other's bodies and the excitement of awakening desire. But they'd enjoyed just being together, too—hiking through the woods, swimming in Town Lake, even reading aloud to each other, corny as that was.

"Life in Cottonwood is good," Luke persisted. "You just have to make your own fun."

Good Lord, he was going to kiss her. Right here on the square, where everyone and their mother could see. As if the town gossips didn't have enough to talk about.

His arms were braced on either side of her, leaning against the car. She bent her knees and ducked out from between them before he could make his own fun.

"Aw, Cindy."

"Luke, even if I were inclined—" and she was, but she didn't want *him* to know that "—it's too soon. Less than two weeks ago I was engaged to another man."

"You were engaged to a fantasy."

"That doesn't make what I felt any less real to me. Give me some time, okay?"

"If I give you time, you're going to be on a plane for Timbuktu!"

"Only if I recover my money before Marvin spends it. And realistically, what are the odds of that?" She reached for her keys inside her purse, but they weren't in their usual spot. With a sinking feeling in the bottom of her stomach, she peered in the window of her car. There were the keys, dangling from the ignition.

She'd never in her life locked her keys in the car. Why now, when all she wanted to do was escape? Luke joined her at the window.

"That's not good."

"Tell me something I don't know."

He sighed. "Wait here." He walked down to where his official SUV was parked, about four spaces from hers. Moments later, he returned with a thin strip of metal. "I'm not really supposed to do this. But since I know you and I know this is your car…"

He slid the metal strip between her car window and the door frame. After a few moments of maneuvering, there was a satisfying click and the door opened.

"There. Now if that had happened in a strange city, who would you have called to help?"

"The rental-car company. The auto club. Traveler's Aide." She climbed into the car and cranked up the engine. "Thank you, Luke. I'll see you later."

She could see Luke in her rearview mirror as she drove off, looking more frustrated than she'd ever seen him. She could understand. She was more than a little frustrated herself.

Luke's shift ended at three, but he was in the midst of dealing with a couple of teenage miscreants intent on defacing a railroad trestle with red spray paint. They were from neighboring Mooresville, a big sports rival with Cottonwood, and the boys had already scrawled school mottoes and a crude drawing of their mascot, a bulldog. But someone had seen and reported them before they'd completed their artwork.

Luke had them sitting on the ground, their hands clasped and on top of their heads, giving them the full arrest treatment. Not only were they defacing public property, they'd skipped school *and* they were drinking. Luke's only comfort was that they weren't Cottonwood kids. He took pictures of the graffiti and the stock of beer they'd been drinking from, then took the beer and spray-paint cans into evidence.

"We'll pay for the damage," one of the boys whined.

"Man, don't tell our parents," said the other, almost in tears.

"If I don't tell your parents, who's going to bail you out of jail?" Luke asked casually as he locked the evidence bags and camera into the back of his Blazer. It was the same exact model as his personal vehicle. Once he found something he liked, he stuck with it.

"We're not really goin' to jail, are we?" said the first one. "For a little spray paint?"

No, Luke didn't want to take them to jail. What he wanted was to scare the bejesus out of them so they wouldn't pull this kind of crap again. So he let them sweat for a while longer. He read them their Miranda rights and watched their eyes get bigger and bigger, then stuffed them into his back seat.

But on the way to the station he cut a deal with them. If they would agree to voluntarily attend an alcohol-abuse program and do about a zillion hours of community service, he'd drop the charges. By the time they repainted the trestle, as well as some bridges and a water tower in their own town, they'd think twice about doing public artwork again.

He drove them all the way back to Mooresville, talked to their parents, got their cooperation. Then he drove back to Cottonwood like a bat out of hell, more anxious than usual to get home. Hell, yeah, he was anxious to see Cindy and Adam again. He'd spent too many years fantasizing about living with Cindy not to enjoy it while he had it.

But he wouldn't repeat the mistake he'd made today. Like it or not, he had to play by her timetable, not his. And of course she needed more time. All he had to do was remember how he'd felt after his breakup with Cindy to realize how unreceptive she must be.

The house was dark and quiet when he arrived home. Where was she? He ran upstairs, worried about what he might find. But all of her things were still there. His breathing returned to normal and he shook his head, disgusted by his own paranoia. He shouldn't let it matter so much. Cindy had dumped him once already. Well, maybe he'd forced her hand by insisting they get married. But she'd walked away from what they'd had with seeming ease, and he didn't kid himself that she couldn't do it again.

He wouldn't put himself through that hell again, he decided more firmly this time. He would do what he could to help Cindy put her life back together. But no more kisses, no more reminders of their teenage romance. She didn't need him pushing any more than he needed to invite that heartache into his life.

The phone rang, breaking into his morose thoughts. When he answered, he found his foster mother on the other end of the line.

"Oh, good, you're finally home," Polly said cheerfully.

"You can always call me on my cell. Or leave a message on my machine." Polly was frankly terrified of any technology developed in the last twenty or thirty years. She always hung up on his answering machine, and she thought cell phones were the devil's work.

"You shouldn't take personal calls when you're working," she said as if this were the first time they'd had this argument. "It wasn't nothin' urgent. But I looked after little Adam today, and when Cindy came to collect him, she ended up pitching in to fix dinner. So, you want to come, too?"

"Does Cindy know you're inviting me?"

"Well, no, but so what?"

"So, she's probably had quite enough of me for one day."

"She'll get over it. Lasagna? With that Italian sausage you like so much? And bread pudding for dessert."

Polly sure knew how to push his buttons.

"Mike's here, too," she continued. "I told him I'd feed him good if he'd fix my porch roof."

"All right, I'll be there."

Cindy wasn't too pleased when Luke showed up for dinner with a bottle of Chianti and a smile. She didn't dare say a word against him in front of Polly, though. His foster mother believed Luke walked on water—in fact, felt that way about all of her chicks. Maybe it was that unwavering faith that made all her foster kids turn out well. And she didn't stand idle while anyone else bad-mouthed them, either.

Not that Cindy could think of anything really bad to say about Luke. He'd been nothing but kind. But she felt a terrible, evil urge to pick a fight with him. Anything to get rid of that warm feeling she got whenever he looked her way and flashed that devilish grin.

She was pleased, though, that Mike was here. Just a year younger than Luke, he'd hung out with them a lot when they were teenagers in a desperate quest to fit in somewhere. Cindy had set him up a zillion times with friends from school, but he'd been kind of scrawny and geeky back then.

Not now. One of his first after-school jobs had

been as a carpenter's apprentice—something Polly had arranged when she'd seen that Mike liked to build things. A few summers of working construction and he'd filled out just fine, with big muscles and curly blond hair liberally streaked by the sun. He had his own construction company now, and all the girls who'd groaned at the idea of dating him back in high school would kill to be seen with him now.

And plenty of them *were* seen with him. A different one every week.

He enveloped her in a bear hug when he came in from working on the porch roof. "You get better-lookin' every day, Miss Cindy."

That was a gift. She knew she looked like hell—too many sleepless nights.

Dinner was a chaotic event, but that was nothing new. Polly's dinner table was where everything got worked out—problems at school, conflicts between the kids, homework issues. Tonight the twins were having a tattlefest on each other and four-year-old Michelle was in tears over missing her mother. Polly poured milk, wiped tears and checked homework all at the same time, while Mike refereed the twins' debate. Five-year-old Ben offered his dubious help in feeding Adam, while Luke answered some questions about law enforcement for eighteen-year-old Bobby, who was having his own crisis about his decision to drop out of high school and attend vo-tech.

"It's never too late to go back," Luke said.

"I'll be a year behind."

"Just means you'll be the biggest, smartest one in the class."

Cindy took it all in. Though the faces changed over the years, Polly's dinner table was a constant.

"Hey, Mike," Luke said in a rare lull in conversation. "I need some work done on my carriage house."

Mike winced. "You guys are going to bankrupt me. Dinners are nice, don't get me wrong, but I need paying customers."

"I never said you had to work for free," Luke said, feigning insult.

"Yeah, but I don't feel right charging family."

"So you'll feel lousy. Charge me the going rate. I need the work done fast. I have a leaking roof in the carriage house and a broken window. The carpeting needs tearing out and replacing."

Mike's ears perked up. "Yeah, I'll do it."

"You gonna warn him about the possums?" Cindy asked. Which prompted much curiosity from the kids, so she and Luke had to recount their close encounter of the rodent kind. Amber laughed so hard, milk came out her nose.

"The possums are no longer a problem," Luke said. "They were evicted earlier today."

"You didn't hurt them, did you?" asked Ben. Cindy had been about to ask the same question. She'd been terrified of the hissing, oversize rats, but she couldn't stand the thought of hurting any animals.

"The pest-control guy said all they had to do was scare them off, then seal up the hole where they were coming and going."

"Oh, good," the little boy said.

"Possums are marsupials, you know," said Ashley. "The only ones native to North America."

"What's a *'supial?*" asked Ben.

"They carry babies in a pouch, like a kangaroo," answered Amber. "We learned about them in science class."

Which provided Polly with a perfect opportunity to query the twins on whether they liked science and whether they might like to be researchers or zoologists when they grew up.

Cindy remembered countless such discussions. Polly never missed an opportunity to help a child discover a hidden passion. A child who became passionate about something—and it could be almost anything, from photography to fishing to physics—was one who would stay out of trouble.

Polly had asked such questions of Cindy herself when Cindy had decided she wasn't going to college. That's when she'd gotten the idea to become a travel agent, which she would have if Jim hadn't come along. That was also when she'd first realized that she didn't have to be stuck in Cottonwood her whole life.

That was also when she'd realized she didn't want to marry right out of high school, as many of her friends were doing.

Luke and Mike were deep into a discussion of the work that needed to be done to the carriage house, and Cindy was frankly surprised. She'd thought Luke would drag his feet, keeping her under his roof for as long as possible.

"I can help clear out the furniture tomorrow," Cindy volunteered. "I certainly don't have anything else to do."

"I guess that means you didn't find a job," said Luke.

"I stopped in at every restaurant within a fifty-mile radius," she said glumly. "No one is hiring. But maybe there'll be some jobs in tomorrow's paper," she added, not really believing it.

* * *

And she was right. As she fed Adam his breakfast the next morning and perused the want ads in the *Cottonwood Conversation,* she didn't find anything she was remotely qualified for. The Clip 'n' Snip Salon was looking for a new stylist, but she couldn't even style her own hair, much less someone else's. The high school needed a chemistry teacher. Yeah, right. The bank was looking for a certified financial analyst and…wait, here was something she could do. Pizza delivery. It was part-time and the pay was minimum wage and child care would probably cost her more than she earned. But maybe she could work her way up to waitress or pizza cook. She called and left a message.

Mike's truck arrived shortly after nine, filled with building supplies. She resigned herself to a day of hard manual labor—and hunger. Polly had pressed an entire grocery sack full of baby food and two boxes of diapers on her last night, claiming she didn't need it since she didn't have any little ones at the moment. Cindy had had no choice but to accept. Adam had to eat, after all. But she had no food for herself, and she refused to raid Luke's kitchen. He was doing enough for her as it was.

She gathered up Adam and his folding play-pen and went to greet Mike.

To her surprise, Luke was with him, dressed in a pair of ratty jeans and a Texas A&M T-shirt.

"What are you doing here?" she blurted out rather inelegantly.

"Took the day off. I couldn't leave all this fun to you two. Besides, I don't trust this guy around you. I saw the way he was looking at you last night."

Luke was just teasing, of course. There'd never been a bit of chemistry between her and Mike. She felt more big-sisterly toward him than anything. But the fact that Luke was act-ing territorial about her, even in a teasing way, unsettled her.

Mike just rolled his eyes and started unload-ing his truck.

"Guess we better start moving the furniture out," Luke said. "I'm sure Polly could watch Adam if you asked."

"Adam will be fine. He's used to entertaining himself." She set up his playpen in a shady spot well out of the way, gave him a radio, his blanky, some favorite toys, and he was good to go.

They carted box after box of trash from the apartment to the alley—old magazines and books, moldering clothes, sheets and curtains, all of it water- and possum-damaged. They filled half a dozen garbage bags with loose plaster, furniture stuffing and other debris. The furry squatters hadn't exactly been tidy, and even with all the windows open, the smell was hideous.

Maybe she'd gotten it wrong, she considered as she dragged a couple of tattered sofa cushions to the pile of trash they were building in the alley. Luke must want her out of his house pretty badly if he was willing to tackle this disgusting mess and pay his brother good money for supplies and labor. Not to mention he was taking time off from work.

Did she blame him? She'd made it pretty clear she did not want to get back together with him. He probably regretted sticking his neck out for her and just wanted her out of his hair.

"Guess that just leaves the sofa," Cindy said.

"I'll get Mike. It's too heavy for the two of us."

"No, it's not," she argued. "I'm stronger than I look. We can get it."

Luke looked dubious, but he gave her the benefit of the doubt.

And she was strong enough. Or she would have been if she'd had anything to eat that day. They got the smelly sofa halfway out the kitchen door when a wave of dizziness overcame her. She dropped her end of the sofa with a thunk. Next thing she knew, she was flat on her back on the kitchen floor.

Luke was instantly beside her. "Dammit, Cin, I told you the sofa was too much for you. Are you hurt?"

"It wasn't the sofa," she argued weakly. "At least, not directly. I got dizzy for a minute." In truth, she'd fainted. Maybe for only a few seconds, but she didn't remember how she'd gotten to the floor.

"I'm taking you to the hospital."

"No! Luke, that's not necessary. I'm fine, really."

"People don't pass out for no reason."

"I'm just hungry, that's all."

He narrowed his eyes at her. "What did you have for breakfast?"

"I didn't," she admitted. "I'm not much of a breakfast person."

"What?" he yelled. "You can't do hours of hard physical labor with nothing in your stomach. And the hell you're not a breakfast person. I know you. I've seen you put away enough pancakes and eggs to satisfy a couple of lumberjacks."

He helped her to her feet, dusted her off— spending a little too much time dusting off her bottom, she thought, but she let it pass.

"All right, so I should have eaten breakfast. I'll eat something now and I'll be fine."

The sofa sat squarely in the doorway, blocking their exit.

"We can just climb over it," she said.

"You can't climb over anything. You're weak as a kitten." With that, he scooped her up, threw her over his shoulder in a fireman's carry and clamored over the sofa.

"Luke, put me down!" she sputtered indignantly. This reminded her far too much of the way they used to horseplay when they were teenagers. Back then, she'd reveled in his strength, in how he could pick her up as if she weighed nothing. Even as she'd squealed for him to put her down, she'd loved the feel of his strong arms around her legs, his hand on her butt and her view of his strong back muscles.

The memories came back to her in a flash, so vivid she almost passed out again. Suddenly she was seventeen again and hopelessly in love.

She didn't need this. She wiggled in earnest as Luke made it to the landing. "Luke, I mean it. Put me down."

She must have accidentally knocked him

off balance, because he went down. The rickety railing around the stair landing was the only thing that kept them from plunging to the ground below. Instead, they landed in a tangle of arms and legs.

"You couldn't just be still for one more second?" Still, Luke didn't make any attempt to climb off her. His face was very close, and she could actually feel his heartbeat through his chest, hard and fast. Like hers.

Cindy closed her eyes, helpless to resist. His lips descended, and she felt caught up in a whirlwind of passion—remembered teenage passion, but it was all mixed up with something different, something deeper and definitely adult.

Dimly she was aware of someone clearing their throat. A female someone. Her eyes flew open and Luke pulled away abruptly. That was when they both saw the woman standing halfway up the stairs, holding Adam in her arms.

Beverly Hicks.

Chapter Seven

Cindy had completely forgotten that the woman had threatened—no, promised, she corrected herself—to return and check out Adam's new living conditions. And she finds Adam alone in his playpen and his purported parents playing a game of slap and tickle on the stairs.

"This isn't what it looks like," Luke said hastily as he extricated himself from Cindy.

"I fainted," Cindy said at the same time. "The door was blocked and Luke was—"

But Beverly was smiling. In fact, she was close to bursting out laughing, Cindy thought.

"Good morning to you, too," Beverly said.

"Is this your new home?" She gave the aging carriage house a doubtful look.

"It will be when we get it fixed up a bit," Cindy explained. "Meanwhile, I'm living in the big house. If you're worried about Adam being left alone in his playpen, I've been just a few feet away the whole time, checking on him about every five—"

Beverly shook her head. "I confess, I was watching from the driveway for a few minutes. I saw you were checking on him often. I just picked him up because he held out his arms to me. He's certainly a trusting child."

Cindy didn't bother to explain that he'd had dozens of caregivers over the past few months. All of her former employees and half the customers had taken turns holding him and feeding him.

"Come on in the house," Luke said, still supporting Cindy down the stairs. "You can look around while I get Cindy something to eat."

"I can get my own—" Cindy started to protest, but Luke hushed her with a stern look. She supposed he was right. She'd proved herself pitifully incapable of taking care of herself.

Beverly took a quick tour of the downstairs, peeking in all the cupboards and the refrigerator, noting all the childproofing Luke had done, then headed upstairs to inspect Adam's quarters.

Luke slammed a glass of juice in front of Cindy. "Start on that. I'll fix you some toaster waffles." He put the waffles in, then got out a jar of peanut butter and one of honey.

He remembered. After all this time, he remembered how she liked to eat her waffles.

Beverly came downstairs frowning. "You need a baby gate for the stairs. And one of the windows is missing a screen. Do you know how many children fall out open windows—"

"We'll take care of it today," Luke assured her.

Beverly relaxed somewhat. "I know I seem like a nitpicker, but when you've seen as many awful things as I have…"

Cindy was too busy stuffing her face with waffles to reply, but Luke did it for her. "We understand."

"Has Adam been seeing a doctor?"

"He gets regular checkups, but he's never been sick a day in his life," Cindy said. She privately thought he was so healthy because he'd been exposed to lots of people as an infant and developed all the antibodies he needed. But she couldn't prove it, so she didn't bring it up.

Satisfied, Beverly left them with some pamphlets on how to create a toddler-safe space, guidelines on a healthy diet and a schedule of when he needed various immunizations. Cindy tried not to be insulted. She might have shortcomings, but she was a good mother, even if she'd been a bit reluctant about it in the beginning.

"Feeling better?" Luke asked, his voice gentle with concern, after she'd polished off three waffles, a glass of juice and some milk.

"I'm fine now, really."

"I think you should rest for a while."

"I can't let you and Mike do all the work."

"Why not? It's my carriage house. You won't be living there that long if your plans work out." There was almost a challenge in his voice as he said this last part, as if he didn't really believe she would carry through with her dreams. She'd been feeling charitable toward him until that moment. Now she hardened herself.

"How about if I go to the hardware store and buy some paint? The whole place needs it." And she needed some distance from Luke Rheems after that potent kiss. He was driving her crazy.

"Okay. Pick out whatever colors you like. I'll watch Adam."

* * *

The phone rang moments after Cindy left. He should probably let the machine get it, Luke thought. He was on call, but if it was anything important, the office would page him. Still, he welcomed a chance to delay his next task, ripping out that mildewed carpet. So he answered.

"This is Reggie from the Pizza Palace over in Mooresville. Is there a Cindy Lefler there?"

"Is this regarding a job?" Luke asked.

"Yeah, delivery. I got an opening starting next week. It's just part-time."

"I'll have her call you." He took down the number, uneasy at the thought of Cindy taking on such a job. It wouldn't pay much. And it wasn't safe for a woman to make pizza deliveries. Hell, it wasn't safe for anyone. Luke had just read a report from Tyler about a guy who'd gotten mugged and beaten while making some type of food delivery.

Luke threw himself into the difficult task of ripping out carpet, but it wasn't nearly as fun without Cindy there. He'd enjoyed working as a team with her, laughing over the odd things they'd found in his long-neglected carriage house, like the stack of ancient *Playboy* magazines the previous tenant had left behind.

He'd enjoyed seeing her face flushed with

the effort of hard work, wisps of her honey-gold hair escaping from her ponytail to tease her nose. He'd especially enjoyed throwing her over his shoulder the way he used to do.

He still had it bad for Cindy. He'd managed to put his desire for her on the back burner for a lot of years, when she'd been married to another man—his friend, no less. But now, all those adolescent yearnings were back full force, mixed in with a healthy dose of fully adult passion.

She wanted him, too. If he could just get it out of her mind that she wanted to leave Cottonwood, purge that wanderlust out of her system. He'd thought maybe all those years of vagabond trucking would have cured her. But all that traveling had only strengthened her desire for adventure and the thrill of strange places.

He'd never understood it, but he'd accepted it as part of what made Cindy Cindy. Now, however, she had a child. He had to make her understand that putting down roots would be the best thing for Adam. Clearly the child was her first priority; she had no qualms about starving herself, but Adam was always bathed and clothed and fed. He'd bet she was religious about his medical checkups, even if she hadn't seen a doctor herself since she'd left the maternity ward.

Adam was the key; he was convinced of that. If Luke could get Adam rooted here in Cottonwood, surely Cindy wouldn't rip out those roots to go wandering about the world.

That's what the carriage house was all about, he thought as he yanked on a particularly stubborn carpet tack with a pair of pliers. To the casual observer, it might look as if he were anxious to get Cindy out from under his roof, but that wasn't it at all. He'd have been thrilled to have her stay there indefinitely.

But she would never consent to that. He figured if he got her her own place and let her fix it up the way she wanted it, she would be less anxious to flee. If she chose the paint and the furnishings, she would have something invested in it. It was much harder to walk away from a place you created than someone else's impersonal white walls.

He also needed to figure out how to find Cindy a job, and not delivering pizza, either. She needed a job she would enjoy, something she wouldn't want to escape from.

Of course, she didn't *have* to work, he thought as he carried an armload of stinky carpet to the alley. His job paid him well enough that it wouldn't be a problem supporting Cindy and Adam. But she wouldn't stand for that very long. And if she couldn't find a job here, she might get it in her head to move to Tyler or even Dallas, where the employment opportunities were more plentiful. She couldn't count on ever recovering her nest egg.

He had a few other ideas on how to keep her in Cottonwood. They were a little on the sneaky side but, as he kept reminding himself, all was fair in love and war. His relationship with Cindy was a little bit of both.

"I'm back." It was Cindy's cheerful voice as her footsteps thumped up the stairs. She had a gallon of paint dangling from each hand.

"Great. What color did you get?"

"I thought you would want something neutral so you could rent it out after I'm gone. I got white."

White? "I told you to pick out a color you liked."

She shrugged. "I like white just fine. It goes with everything, right?"

This wasn't working out exactly as planned. He'd forgotten to take something into account. Cindy was not a nester. Now that he thought about it, the walls in her house had been white, too, and the carpeting institutional beige. And he couldn't recall seeing many pictures on the walls or knickknacks on the shelves. She'd walked away from that house without a backward glance, hadn't regretted anything except leaving behind some practical things, like Adam's crib.

This was going to be harder than he'd thought.

"Don't put down your purse. We're going shopping."

"What? What do we need? I can go get it."

"We'll pick up some lunch while we're out," he said, ignoring her objection. "Mike is probably starving."

"O-okay." Cindy set down the paint.

Luke immediately picked it up again.

"What are you doing?" she asked, bewildered.

"We're returning this paint. I want you to pick out a color you like."

"But what if the next person who lives here doesn't have my taste? I'll only be here a short time."

Luke gritted his teeth. "I'm not planning to rent it out after you're gone. Now come on."

He remembered about Cindy's phone message from the pizza place after they were in her car and on the way to town. She couldn't call back about the job while they were out, he reasoned. He'd tell her when they got back.

* * *

Buell's Hardware was just a block off the square, in one of the oldest buildings in Cottonwood. The store itself was long and narrow, with pine plank floors, narrow aisles and shelves stuffed and stacked full of the most amazing things, all the way up to the pressed-tin ceiling. Though it was a third the size of the modern hardware store on the edge of town, it seemed to have everything any do-it-yourselfer could dream of.

Cindy could remember coming here with her father when she was little. It was a wonderland of strange gadgets and esoteric tools, more fun than a toy store, though she was about the least handy person in the world. She could do routine maintenance on a diesel truck, but she was hopeless at home improvement.

Luke, Cindy and Adam made their way to the back of the store, where the paint department was. It featured a rack of color chips in every hue of the rainbow and an ancient paint-mixing machine.

"Now," Luke said, "pick a color."

"White was fine," she groused.

"White is boring. I want you to pick out something that you'll enjoy waking up to every day. You can pick out some different colors if you want—one for the bedroom, one for the main room, one for the kitchen, the bath—"

"Luke, I'm having enough trouble with just one color." She had no earthly idea what would look good. Yellow, maybe? Yellow was cheerful, and that's what Luke had chosen for his guest room. Or maybe orange. Adam loved orange.

"How about this one?" She pointed to a pumpkin-colored card.

"Uh, that's a bold choice." She could tell he hated it.

"Well, don't tell me to choose and then second-guess me. What about this one?" She pointed to a lemon-yellow card.

"No, we'll go with your first choice. Whatever you want."

"Sure you don't want white?" she asked. "Last chance."

Luke plucked the pumpkin card from its holder and handed it to Mr. Buell, the store owner. "Two gallons of this, please."

Mr. Buell's bushy eyebrows shot up. "You sure?"

Cindy started to object, but Luke overruled her. "We're sure. We want to return this white, too."

"Okay, Luke."

"You stay and wait for the paint," Luke said to Cindy. "I'll run over to Triple G Barbecue and get us some lunch."

She nodded, thinking he'd gotten pretty bossy all of a sudden. But, shoot, maybe she needed someone to boss her around. She obviously was no good at making decisions for herself. She couldn't do something as simple as picking out paint without messing it up. She hoped the pumpkin paint wouldn't be too awful.

Adam had wandered over to a display of paint brushes and had systematically pulled every one from its hook and hurled it to the floor. Cindy patiently put them all back, letting him "help."

"What a mess you made," she said fondly. "Now we get to clean it up, nice and neat."

"Say, that looks better than before," said the patient Mr. Buell. "You just let that little tot mess up anything he wants."

That gave Cindy an idea. "Say, Mr. Buell, you don't need any help around here, do you? Someone to sweep up, straighten the shelves, that sort of thing?"

"I sure could," he said enthusiastically. But then he quickly added, "But I can't afford help. I do all right with this little store, but not well enough to pay an employee."

Cindy sighed. "It's been a tough year for everyone, I guess, with the tornado and all." A few months earlier, a tornado had taken out an entire block of storefronts right across the street from the hardware store, which had become a temporary clinic to treat the injured.

"Didn't you do a lot of business after the tornado, though?" Cindy asked. "With everyone rebuilding…"

"Oh, yeah, a lot of business. On credit. If I could collect what I'm owed, I'd be a rich man."

He wouldn't, though. Mr. Buell had always been lax about credit. He hadn't batted an eye when she'd come in earlier today to buy paint and hadn't had a dime to her name.

She signed another sales ticket now, though she imagined Luke intended to pay for it. She let Mr. Buell watch Adam a few minutes while she loaded the paint into her trunk. Then she collected the baby and went looking for Luke.

The town of Smoky Bayou, Louisiana, turned out to be a little bigger than Sonya and Brenna had guessed, but they could still drive from end to end in about three minutes. They spent an hour or so investigating every side street, looking for Marvin's yellow Porsche. But they saw no sign of it.

"Guess we should start asking questions," Brenna said.

"I hope we don't find another Cindy."

"What did you think of her, anyway?"

Sonya thought for a moment. "Seemed like a nice enough person. But she's got a long battle ahead of her."

"Yeah. At least Marvin didn't sell my loft out from under me. And I still have my jewelry business, even if he did swipe almost all my inventory. I was getting ready for a jewelry show next month."

"Your business is your talent, and no one can take that from you."

Brenna smiled. "Thanks, Sonya. I needed to hear that."

"I wish I had a talent like yours."

"Everyone has a talent."

"I don't. My entire life, I was groomed for one thing only—snag a rich husband and be the perfect wife."

"Martha Stewart turned that into a multibillion-dollar empire."

"I can't cook. I plan menus and give them to servants. Anyway, back to Cindy. She's got more problems than finding a place to live. There's the deputy."

"What's wrong with him? He seemed decent enough."

"Oh, he's decent, all right. He's also in love with Cindy."

"Well, duh. Anyone with two eyes could see that. You think that's a problem?"

"How would you feel if a gorgeous man started paying attention to you?"

"I'd think he was after my money. The money I no longer have. But Cindy doesn't have any money."

"Doesn't matter. She still won't trust any man within a hundred yards of her."

"But she's known Luke all her life, hasn't she?"

"True. But maybe it's not Luke she doesn't trust. She had the most wary eyes of any woman I've ever seen."

"Have you looked in the mirror lately? You counted your change three times at Dairy Queen, positive that teenager behind the register had shortchanged you."

Sonya firmed her mouth. "This isn't about me."

"Everything's about you, Sonya." She'd meant

it as a teasing quip, but it came out more mean-spirited than that, and Sonya fell silent.

Now Brenna felt guilty. "I didn't mean that, really. You've been very generous, putting everything on your credit card."

"No, you're right. I'm incredibly self-centered. If I saw something in Cindy that bothered me, it's probably because I see it in myself. I've spent my whole life distrusting men and their motives. And the one time I let my guard down was probably the one time I should have been most suspicious."

"Marvin's good. We've established that. Don't beat yourself up."

Sonya pulled their rental car into a parking space at a strip shopping center.

"Why are we stopping here?" Brenna asked.

"I need a manicure."

"We're trying to catch a con man, and you're worried about your nails?"

"Well, look at them!" She displayed her shiny, pink-frosted nails for Brenna's inspection. Her left pinkie had one tiny chip, but otherwise they looked perfect. Brenna wanted to hide her own bitten nails.

"God, what an embarrassment. Of course we should spend an hour getting you a manicure, never mind that we might be within spitting distance of Marvin right this minute."

"I'll only be twenty minutes," Sonya promised. "Meanwhile, you can start asking around at these other little shops. But be discreet. We don't want to flush him out until we're ready."

Brenna spotted a tattoo-and-piercing salon down the row from the nail place. "Nah, I think I'll go get something pierced instead."

Sonya looked revolted, as Brenna had expected. Inwardly Brenna laughed. She liked Sonya, she really did. Considering how different they were, they got along pretty well as traveling companions. Brenna supposed their shared purpose kept them from getting too mad at each other.

She hoped they found Marvin soon, though. They'd been on the road for almost two weeks, during which she hadn't even spoken to her family or friends or neighbors back in Dallas. She'd made up a story about an impromptu vacation, unwilling to let anyone know the depth of her stupidity.

Sonya's situation was even worse. She'd been planning a wedding and she hadn't yet called it off. To hear Sonya tell it, her mother was like a runaway train with the wedding plans, and she probably hadn't even noticed Sonya was gone.

At least Cindy had already faced the worst. Brenna suspected she and Sonya were only delaying their ugly fates.

Chapter Eight

"You've got paint on your nose."

"What? Oh, no." Cindy sighed. "I'm just not very good at this, am I?" This was their second day working on the carriage house's interior while Mike worked on the roof, windows, doors and rotted wood siding. She and Luke had cleaned all day yesterday. This morning, Cindy had crawled out of bed, every muscle aching from the unaccustomed physical labor. But oddly, she'd hurried through her shower and breakfast, eager to get back to it. It was kind of fun seeing the tiny apartment improve hour by hour and being a part of the team that made it happen.

They'd patched holes and cracks in the walls and woodwork for a couple of hours this morning. Then they'd started in with the paint—which in bright daylight was undeniably orange.

Cindy had made a terrible choice, she realized, but she wasn't going to back down from it now. Luke wouldn't be able to get his money back for the custom-mixed paint, so she was going to learn to love it. She consoled herself that Adam would like it—if she could manage to get the stuff onto the walls rather than on herself.

Luke handed her a damp rag, and she scrubbed at her nose. "Did I get it?"

"Not quite." He took the rag from her, then held her chin to steady her face and rubbed gently at her nose. "You've got some here, too." He rubbed a spot on her cheek.

"I might as well take a bath in the stuff." She felt suddenly warm, and not just from the exertion of painting. Why did he have to stand so close? She'd been doing her best to tamp down her feelings for Luke, not trusting herself one inch. She was needy and vulnerable, just as she'd been after Jim's and her mother's deaths, and she would probably feel warm toward any man who showed her kindness. That was no basis on which to form a relationship, as she'd so harshly discovered.

Warm was a mild way of describing her growing feelings for Luke. He was so strong, so sure of himself. He always seemed to have an answer for everything. And yet, with Adam he was sweet and gentle as a dandelion. And Adam adored Luke, clinging to him every chance he got. He'd even called Luke "Da-da" one time, although it was probably only an accident of diction.

But Adam loved everyone, she reminded herself. He'd loved Dex. *Marvin.* The con man had used Adam shamelessly to get to Cindy and, boy, had it worked. She was a sucker where her child was concerned. She needed to be very, very careful that she didn't fall for Luke simply because he was kind to her son.

She pulled away from Luke as quickly as she could without looking like a scared rabbit. "Thank you, I'm sure that's fine. What are we going to do about the trim?" The windows, door frames and baseboards were all a dingy white, though much of the paint was cracked and peeling. "Can we just paint over them?"

Luke shuddered. "They'll have to be scraped and sanded. And we'll need a different paint."

"How about yellow?" She was heady with

the concept of picking out colors, even if she was bad at it.

Luke winced. "How about that nice white you were so crazy about earlier?"

"Okay." Why was white too boring for the walls but perfectly acceptable for the trim? This was a game in which she didn't understand the rules. "Hey, since I'm not much good at this painting stuff, why don't I try the scraping and sanding? I did some work like that on the boat when I was a kid. As I recall, it was the only thing my father trusted me to do."

Luke embraced that idea wholeheartedly. Anything to get that paint brush out of her hands, she supposed. He set her up in the adjoining room, so the dust wouldn't settle in the wet paint, with a scraper and a small palm sander. It was hard, messy work, but she enjoyed watching the dirty white paint disappear. She liked the feel of the smooth wood after she sanded. And she especially liked the distance from Luke, so she could get her head on straight once more.

They broke for lunch, and Polly brought over thick po'boy sandwiches and potato salad. Michelle and Ben were thrilled to have Adam to play with, dragging him around as if he were a live baby doll. Adam reveled in the attention, squealing with laughter as they all rolled across the lawn in a squirming lump-o-child.

Then Cindy realized she'd heard another noise, a different kind of high-pitched whine, coming from under one of the bushes that lined Luke's driveway. She went to investigate and, to her surprise, found a shivering puppy with black fur and floppy ears. It couldn't have been more than a couple of months old.

Cindy coaxed it out. Once it realized she didn't want to kick it or eat it, it galloped toward her on clumsy puppy feet, overjoyed when she scooped it up.

"Look what I found!" she announced to Luke, Mike and Polly, who were sitting at a picnic table on the patio eating the last of their lunch.

"Oh, how cute!" Polly immediately held out her hands to the puppy, who went as willingly as Adam did.

"Where'd he come from?" Mike asked.

"He was hiding under that bush over there. He must have wandered away from his home and gotten lost."

"I can't think of anyone around here who's had a litter of puppies recently," said Luke, taking a closer look at the puppy. "Looks like a Labrador retriever."

"Not pure-blooded, I don't think." Mike would know, since he owned several purebred black Labs. "He might have a little something else mixed in."

The kids spotted the puppy before long and came over to investigate, and within a few minutes the puppy was frolicking with the children.

"You don't suppose he has any diseases, do you?" Cindy asked with belated concern.

"Oh, he looked pretty healthy to me," Luke drawled. "You're probably right—he must have wandered off from his home."

"We should try to find out where he belongs. His owners might be frantic about him."

"We'll ask around the neighborhood," said Luke, seemingly unconcerned.

They all enjoyed a few more minutes of downtime. It was an idyllic moment, Cindy thought, something out of a storybook. Families together, perfect fall weather, a heavenly picnic lunch complete with lemonade, the sound of children laughing and the happy yips of the puppy.

Something shifted in Cindy's chest as she realized this wasn't something she'd experienced very often in her life. Her parents had been good people but very serious. They'd worked long hours and expected the same from Cindy.

Since all they did was cook and serve food at work, preparing meals at home had been a chore, never a joy. The boat had been their only attempt at a leisure activity, but even that had ended up being more work than fun.

She could get used to this, Cindy mused. And when she realized where her mind was taking her, she was shocked. No, no, no, this is all wrong. She wasn't the sort of person who enjoyed family get-togethers and block parties and kids' birthdays—and puppies, for heaven's sake. She craved adventures, breathtaking scenery, the open road, sleeping in a different environment every night.

A wave of melancholy washed over her, strong enough to obliterate the momentary pleasure she'd felt. She missed traveling. The ache of losing Jim, which had been numbed into submission while she'd been gaga over Dex/Marvin, returned, though the pain was more poignant and bittersweet than before.

Her feet were absolutely itching. She had to get away, even if it was only for a weekend, just to remember what it was like. Before she let herself get sucked into another homey scene like this one.

She stood abruptly. "We really should get back to work. Thanks so much, Polly, for bringing the food and the kids over. I've never seen Adam have so much fun."

"You're very welcome," Polly replied, beaming. "Adam is such a sunny little boy. I suspect he makes his own fun wherever he goes. What are you going to do with the puppy?"

Good question. The poor little beast had flopped down in exhaustion on a sunny patch of grass, and Adam had stretched out next to it, one arm draped possessively over his new friend. He was ready for a nap.

"I guess we can keep it in the backyard until we find the owner," Luke said, trying to make it sound like a hardship. But she'd seen the laughter in his eyes as he'd watched the puppy and the children cavort. He'd had a dog when he'd lived with Polly, she recalled—a big, floppy mutt named Buddy.

"What happened to Buddy?" Cindy asked.

"Aw, Buddy," the other three adults said together with the same degree of fondness.

"Man, what a great dog," said Mike. "He died, gosh, must have been six or seven years ago."

"While you were on the road," Luke added.

"That Buddy healed many a heart," said Polly. "He always knew which child was hurting, even if they didn't show it on the outside.

He licked away more tears and always managed to be a pal to the kid who needed him most."

"I remember he came to me that first night I stayed with you, Polly," Luke said. "He crawled right into bed with me."

"Maybe if we can't find this little one's home, you should keep it," Cindy suggested.

"Oh, I already have a puppy," Polly said. "Mike's dog had a litter and he gave me one. Looks a lot like this one, in fact."

"I'm sure we'll find his family," Luke said, nodding toward the softly snoring puppy.

"Her family," Mike corrected him. "It's a girl dog."

Adam, not quite asleep, sat up and thumped on the puppy's side with his hand. "Doggy," he said clear as day.

"Did you hear that?" Cindy said excitedly. "That wasn't random. He's really talking! Oh, I thought I'd never see the day."

"Doggy," Adam said again, giggling at his mother's reaction.

Cindy picked up her son and twirled him around. "That's right. *Doggy*."

"Doggy" and Adam alternately played and slept together the rest of the afternoon as Luke, Cindy and Mike continued work on the carriage house. Though she was exhausted, Cindy offered to fix dinner. Cooking was, after all, the one thing she excelled at. Luke put a makeshift collar and leash on the puppy, and he and Adam went up and down the street and around the block trying to find Doggy's home. They returned an hour later, defeated. No one had seen the puppy before.

"You don't suppose someone dumped him, do you?" Cindy asked, disgusted at the idea.

"Unfortunately, people do that all the time, especially in this neighborhood, where there are lots of kids."

"That's horrible. Well, I'm sure we can find her a good home. She's cute and obviously great with children."

"Maybe I'll keep her," Luke said.

"You can't do that, Luke. You're at work all day. A puppy needs people around. Kids, especially."

He didn't argue further, and she figured she'd gotten through to him.

"That dinner sure smells good," Luke commented as he set the table.

"It's just baked chicken, corn bread and green beans."

"Mmm, just like at the Miracle Café. Say,

maybe since you're having trouble finding a job, you could open your own restaurant."

"Hah! And be tied to it night and day? No, thanks."

"I don't know, Cin. You shouldn't throw out the suggestion without thinking about it. Folks around here are going into withdrawal without their Miracle biscuits and gravy. And no one could do a better chicken-fried steak."

Cindy knew he was only trying to help, but the idea appalled her. She'd spent so much of her life planning and plotting to escape from the café. Why would she willingly put herself in that position again? "Not gonna happen," she said mildly, refusing to let him irk her.

As she was putting dinner on the table, she noticed a scrap of paper sitting on the counter, under the phone. She paused, a plate of corn bread in one hand, a bowl of green beans in the other, to read what it said.

She almost dropped the food. "The guy from the pizza place called?" she asked, her voice going shrill.

"Oh, yeah, that's right. I almost forgot to give you that."

"Almost?" Cindy repeated incredulously. She set the food down on the table with a thud. "When did he call?"

"Oh…the other day. When you were at the hardware store." At least he had the good grace to look guilty.

"Luke, that call was about a job! He's the only person to show even mild interest in hiring me, and you *almost forgot* to tell me?"

"I'm sorry, Cindy, really. It slipped my mind."

"It's only a part-time delivery job, but I figure I could move up, maybe to the kitchen. I know how to bake pizza." She went to the old wall phone and began dialing the number Luke had written down.

She asked for the manager, who was thankfully still there. "Oh, Ms. Lefler, hi. I'm sorry, but I just hired someone else for the position. Keep checking back with us, though. We get a lot of turnover."

"I'll keep that in mind. Thanks." She hung up the phone and turned murderous eyes on Luke. "He just filled the job. If you'd given me the message in a timely fashion, that job might have been mine."

Luke shrugged helplessly. "I'm sorry, really. But you don't really want a job as a pizza-delivery girl, do you?"

"Is it a job? Does it have a paycheck? Yes, of course I wanted it. I'm broke and desperate, or hadn't you noticed?"

"You don't have to be desperate. I already told you, you're welcome here as long as you need. Take your time, get a job you really want."

"News flash—there *is* no job I really want. When I do get a job, it'll be to keep body and soul together until I can figure out a new plan for my life. So I don't care what it is. Pizza delivery is fine."

"It's dangerous for a woman alone."

"Life is a series of risks." She yanked out her chair and sat down. "We better eat before it gets cold."

Dinner was a tense affair, and Luke didn't know how to bring things back to normal. He supposed he didn't blame Cindy for being angry, though he hadn't forgotten the message on purpose. Still, maybe subconsciously he'd been trying to orchestrate Cindy's life. He certainly wasn't above subterfuge. The little mutt wiggling around his ankles was ample proof of his deviousness.

Polly had almost blown it. Her puppy and this one were in fact littermates. Mike's prize Labrador bitch had jumped a fence and come home two days later in a family way, so he was trying to find homes for the little mutts. Luke had thought it would be good for Adam to have a dog to play with, but he'd known Cindy would object. So he'd hidden the pup under a bush and waited for Cindy to "discover" it.

Just seeing Adam and the puppy rolling around together convinced him he'd done the right thing, though Cindy wouldn't agree. A dog was just something to tie her down; that was what she'd say.

Now he was left with how to smooth things over with her about the job. He had an idea, though. If he helped her find another job, that ought to convince her he wasn't really trying to keep her from being independent. He wanted her strong and self-reliant and happy. He just wanted her to be all those things in Cottonwood, where Adam could grow up with roots and values and a sense of community and a positive male influence.

"Do you have to work tomorrow?" Cindy asked, apparently making her own attempt to gloss over their disagreement.

"No. I took a week of vacation."

"You're wasting vacation time with a home-improvement project?"

He shrugged. "What else would I do?"

"Go somewhere! Take a trip!"

"I can't think of anywhere I really want to go."

Cindy looked appalled. "Have you ever been out of Texas?"

"Yes, as a matter of fact."

"When? Where?"

"You don't believe me?"

"I don't think you'd lie. I just want to know details." She had eaten most of her own dinner and now had Adam in her lap, coaxing him to try some mashed-up green beans. Luke realized Cindy needed a high chair. Maybe Polly had one of those, too.

"I was born in Louisiana," he said. "But my mother moved to Houston before I was two, so I don't remember it."

"That's it?"

"Some people don't need to travel. I have everything I need right here."

"How would you know if you've never tried anything else?"

"I've tried a lot of things." His tone of voice indicated he wanted to close the subject. She had no idea the sights and sounds he'd experienced before moving to Cottonwood. It was something he never spoke of and tried not to even think about.

He could tell she didn't understand his need for structure and routine and continuity any more than he understood her call to adventure.

For the first time ever, it occurred to him that he and Cindy might not be compatible enough to be a couple. He'd always known they had this one basic difference, but he'd assumed they could overcome it. That she'd learn to settle down like everyone else. Now he wasn't so sure.

It was a sobering realization.

Still, he wasn't giving up. He intended to give her every opportunity to convert to his way of thinking, especially where Adam was concerned. They had that goal in common, at least—putting Adam's welfare first. Now they just had to agree on the best way to do that.

Chapter Nine

Cindy had to admit she was enjoying herself. For three days, she and Luke had worked feverishly on the carriage house—scraping and sanding and painting, hanging curtains, replacing broken light fixtures and missing doorknobs and faceplates for the electrical outlets. Mike had installed new carpeting in a nice oatmeal color. By the time they'd moved in furniture—mostly hers, filled in with a few extras from Luke's and Polly's and Mike's garages and attics—and hung a few pictures, the pumpkin walls were starting to look better to her.

"I've never lived in a place this nice," she said sheepishly as she and Luke carried her few personal belongings into the bedroom. "You could get a really nice rent for this apartment now."

"I'll be glad to collect rent from you, once you get a job."

She was somewhat relieved to hear that. She'd been shamelessly eating Luke's food and sleeping under his roof. She didn't like filling the role of charity case, and she silently vowed she would repay him somehow.

When she got her money back, she reminded herself.

"Say, Luke, have you had any luck tracking down information about Marvin? You said you had a couple of contacts...."

He frowned as he lowered his tall frame to sit on the edge of Cindy's bed. "I made some phone calls, but Brenna was right. It's hard to light a fire under anyone at the national level when Marvin isn't a murderer or kidnapper or terrorist. But I did make sure Marvin's vital statistics were listed on the NCIC computer—that's a national law enforcement database. If he commits similar crimes elsewhere—"

"He will," Cindy interjected. She continued to hang her meager wardrobe in the closet while they talked.

"Right now, the best we can do is try to connect his crimes and figure out a pattern."

Cindy sighed. "Thanks for trying. I talked to Brenna and Sonya earlier today. They've dug up a few leads to follow. I wish I could be with them to help."

Suddenly, Luke's face brightened. "I know you do, honey, but you can't. You have a job."

She dropped a coat hanger, and it clattered to the floor. "Excuse me?"

"Ed LaRue wants to talk to you," Luke said casually, sitting on the edge of her bed.

"Me? What for?"

"He wants to hire you as a manager. It's no secret his new restaurant is failing miserably. Part of the reason is loyalty to you. He figures if he can't beat you, he'll join you. Or rather, convince you to join him."

"How did you learn all this?"

"I ran into him at the post office this morning. I didn't think you'd be interested, but I promised him I'd mention it to you."

"Of *course* I'm interested. It's a job. I'll go over and see him right away." She could stomach anything, even putting up with a boss like Ed LaRue, if it meant a paycheck. She started pawing through her suitcase for something suitable for a job interview, something that wasn't too badly wrinkled. She didn't have an iron.

"Guess I'll leave you to it, then." He stood and turned toward the door, but she stopped him before he could leave.

"Oh, Luke, would you…could you—"

He grinned as if he'd just been waiting for her to bring it up. "I'll be glad to watch Adam. I need to take that puppy to the animal shelter—"

"What?" she shrieked. "Oh, Luke, can't we give it another day or two? I know Doggy's a lot of trouble—"

"Hey, take it easy. I'm just going to get her a checkup and shots. Doc Chandler volunteers at the shelter one day a week, and he donates his fees."

"Oh. Oh, thank goodness." She hadn't realized how attached she'd become to that darn puppy in just a couple of days, and Adam had little interest in anything else. Even now, the puppy was sniffing around the newly refurbished bedroom, checking things out, and Adam was waddling after her like a caboose.

"Cindy, how could you even think I would ever take a puppy to the pound?" Luke asked indignantly.

"Oh, I don't know. You're right, of course.

You'd be much more likely to try to find her a nice family."

"She's already found a nice family."

"Yes, but I can't keep her."

"I can. And I'm going to. Lots of people who work have dogs. It'll be fine." He looked at her, daring her to argue.

She wouldn't dream of arguing. She was secretly thrilled Luke was willing to keep Doggy. "You better take her out before she piddles on this brand-new carpet," she said. The puppy seemed to have received some rudimentary house training before her arrival, but she was far from perfect.

Luke scooped up the puppy with one hand and Adam with the other. "Come on, guys. Mom has to get ready for her job interview. We'll go have us some fun."

Luke had mixed feelings about Cindy working for Ed LaRue. But he'd been asking around every place he could think of and the job market was tight. No one had any openings for someone with Cindy's skills. He'd had to do some fast talking to convince Ed LaRue that hiring Cindy was the only way he could stay in business. He could only hope the guy would be fair to Cindy.

"Is this one of Mike's puppies?" Doc Chandler asked when Luke and Adam came in with their new little friend.

"Uh-huh." He hoped Doc wouldn't spill the beans to Cindy.

"And who's this little tyke? Oh, wait a minute, I know you. You're Adam Lefler. How ya doin', big guy?" Then Doc became suddenly very busy checking the puppy over. Luke hadn't imagined that a man close to seventy could blush. Had he said something wrong?

Doc gave the pup her shots, then filled out the paperwork for her dog license. "What's her name?"

"Er, Doggy."

"Doggy!" Adam repeated gleefully.

"What can I say? Adam chose the name."

"It's a fine name," Doc said generously. Luke bought a truckload of pet supplies from the animal shelter's store—bowls and food and treats and flea drops and a bed and collar and leash. The list went on, and he'd spent a fortune by the time he walked out of that place.

He stopped at the hardware store for a few odds and ends, where he met the same embarrassed stuttering from Mr. Buell as he'd gotten from Doc Chandler. What was going on?

When he walked through the town square

with Adam on his hip, he got stares and a couple of smirks, as well as several people who wouldn't meet his gaze.

Okay, this was getting ridiculous. But he knew just the person who could clear things up for him. Margie Blankenship at Tri-County Realty was the biggest gossip in town. She couldn't keep a secret if her life depended on it.

He stopped in on the pretext of asking what he might rent a one-bedroom carriage house for. He did need the information so he would know what to reasonably ask Cindy to pay— if they got that far.

Margie, one of the real-estate company's owners and also the office manager, was only too pleased to discuss it with him. She showed him a list of available rentals that were similar in size to his carriage house and how much they were going for, all the while casting sly glances at Adam.

"So, I guess it's true, then," Margie blurted out.

"What?" Luke asked innocently.

"You and Cindy are back together."

"That's not exactly true," Luke said, amazed, though he knew he shouldn't be. Rumors grew and spread in Cottonwood faster than kudzu spread through the woods. "I'm just lending her a hand."

"But I thought... Well, I'd heard... Oh, never mind. I'm sure it's none of my business."

"I'm happy to clear up any misunderstandings," Luke said pleasantly. "What did you hear?"

"That you're Adam's real father. 'Course, I didn't believe that part."

"Oh, holy cow." He'd never imagined his impulsive lie to Beverly Hicks would spread all over town. If Cindy got wind of this, she would be livid! It wasn't just an embarrassing falsehood, it was a grave dishonor to Cindy and her deceased husband.

"I guess that means it's not true."

"Where did you hear it?" Luke asked.

"From Esther Schilling. She cleans Leona Blake's house, and she heard it from Betty Bruno. I don't know where Betty heard it."

From her husband, who worked at the marina and was probably the person who filed the original complaint against Cindy. If he'd called to follow up, he'd probably been assured that Adam's *father* was taking temporary custody— never mind privacy issues.

What a mess.

"Margie," Luke said in as even a tone as

possible, "Adam is Jim Lefler's son." He could only hope the truth didn't filter back to Beverly Hicks. "Cindy is an old friend and I'm helping her out of a jam. That's all."

"Oh." Margie looked supremely disappointed. "I always thought you two made a cute couple when you were kids. Not that I didn't like Jim—everyone liked Jim. But everyone thought you two would get married."

"I did, too," Luke couldn't help saying. "But Cindy had other plans." Just as she had other plans now. "If you hear any further speculation of this nature, would you please set people straight? Cindy would never, ever, in a million years have cheated on her husband. Ever."

"I knew that. Really, I did," Margie said. "But I was still hoping that maybe you two…"

"No." Not yet, anyway.

Cindy was about to burst with her good news and she had no one to tell. When she'd come home from her interview with Ed LaRue, she'd been disappointed that Luke, Adam and Doggy were still gone. And then she realized she really had no other close friends she could tell. Her dearest friends were her former employees— Kate, Iris, Tonya and Manson. And she could hardly call them and brag about her good fortune when they were all still unemployed, and all because of her folly.

She knew they would be happy for her. None of them blamed her personally for Marvin's actions. But working for Ed felt too much as if she was going over to the enemy.

Still, a paycheck was a paycheck.

She was just finishing her unpacking when she heard the hum of Luke's car engine coming up the driveway. She ran all the way down the stairs and greeted him, barraging him before he'd even gotten out of the Blazer.

"Guess what? I have a job!"

Luke grinned as he unfolded his tall, muscular frame from the driver's seat. "With Ed?"

She nodded. "He agreed to hire me as an assistant manager, and he's going to pay me more than I thought possible. Not a fortune, I mean, but enough that Adam and I won't starve to death. I start on Monday. I could have started today, and I probably should have, but I didn't want to look too eager." She realized she was babbling as Luke unfastened the straps on Adam's car seat. The puppy, which had leaped out of the SUV the moment it could, was bounding around Cindy's feet now, begging for attention.

She reached down to scratch Doggy behind her ears and forced herself to slow down. Then she took Adam, who babbled excitedly as if he understood every word she said.

"Oh, Adam, I'll hate being away from you all day. But I already talked to Polly, and she said she'd babysit."

Luke was still grinning. "I'm glad it worked out."

"Oh, you. You set the whole thing up, and don't try to deny it. Ed said you were the one who brought it up, not him."

Luke shrugged. "I don't exactly remember."

"Whatever. Thanks, Luke." She put her free arm around his neck, intending to give him a brief and very nonsexual hug. But his arms went around her and Adam in an automatic reaction, and they didn't let her go. And she didn't exactly struggle to get loose. She kissed his cheek and then just brushed her lips against his. A friendly kiss. No harm in that.

Except then it got a whole lot more serious. Luke kissed her back, and it was no innocent brushing of lips. He covered her mouth with his, pressing firmly, one hand at the back of her head to prevent her escape. As if.

The years disappeared and she was seventeen again, making out with Luke in the back seat or on a picnic blanket in the woods, her body burning with desire and wondering whether they could risk making love again, whether they would get caught or whether she would get pregnant despite the fact that they were careful.

Her legs wobbled from the force of the memory. But rather than run from it, she wanted to sink right into it, lose herself in it. Her heart was pierced with a yearning so strong and sweet, those long-suppressed memories taking control of her body and brain like a fast-growing vine.

Only Adam's squeak of protest brought her back to reality. She and Luke broke off the kiss as they both realized they were squishing poor Adam between them.

Adam. All those years swiftly reinstated themselves. She wasn't seventeen. She was a mature widow who had to stay focused on the practical.

"Cindy..."

"Luke..." she said at the same exact time, and they both laughed, embarrassed.

She pulled all the way out of his embrace, so they were no longer touching at all. "Guess my gratitude knows no bounds," she said, trying to make a joke, but it fell flat.

"That was a long time coming."

"It shouldn't have come at all," she said decisively. "Luke, you know I'm in no position to…to…"

"To what? Show affection?"

"It's not just that and you know it. I've recently come out of a relationship that ended about as badly as any relationship can end. And before that, I was widowed. Clearly I'm not in the healthiest frame of mind to make decisions about men or relationships of any kind." Adam asked to be put down with Doggy. She walked over to the gate in the chain-link fence and let them both into the yard. The two of them immediately began rolling around together.

"I'm not asking for any monumental decisions," Luke said. "It was just a kiss."

"Yeah, the kind of kiss that leads to other things. It's those other things I'm not ready to tackle." And he knew exactly what she was talking about. She could tell by the way he wouldn't meet her gaze.

"Just because two men have left you—in vastly different ways, I might add—doesn't mean the next one will. I'm not going anywhere."

"But I am. Luke, get real. It would be stupid for me to start something I couldn't finish. My future is so uncertain right now. And I don't trust myself to act sensibly. I mean, clearly

I left my good judgment at the dry cleaner's when I got mixed up with Marvin. Obviously I'm still not acting sensibly."

"You can't equate me with Marvin."

"No, I didn't mean anything of the sort. Just—we hurt each other once. I wouldn't want to… I need time, Luke. I told you that before. I have enough on my plate."

"If I give you any more time, you'll be gone. By the time your good judgment returns, you'll be in Saskatchewan or Madagascar, and some other guy will snag you." He said this lightly, but Cindy detected the tension beneath the words.

"So you're going to 'snag' me, as you put it, before I have a chance to put my dreams into action."

"I don't want to stop anyone from living their dreams," he said defensively.

"Yes, you do. Oh, my gosh, that's what this is all about. The apartment, the job. Here I thought you were wanting to help me become independent, and really you're trying to tie me down to Cottonwood."

From the way he flinched, she guessed she'd hit a nerve. Damn him, that was exactly what he was trying to do.

"And was that what the kiss was about, too?

If I have a local boyfriend, I won't want to run all over the world with Adam?"

"Hey, who started the kiss?"

All right, maybe she'd taken her accusations too far. Not everyone was scheming and calculating like Marvin. And she had initiated the kiss, though Luke was the one who'd turned it into something it shouldn't have become.

She took a deep breath. She didn't want to fight with Luke. "I'll make you a deal. You give me some room. Recognize the fact that I'm weak and vulnerable where men are concerned and don't take advantage of it. And I'll stop searching for hidden motives in everything you do."

"I want you, Cindy. It's part of who I am."

"It was a high-school romance. We should be able to put it behind us, don't you think?"

Just then there was a commotion in the yard. Cindy looked to see Doggy running around the yard with a huge uprooted vine in her mouth. At the end of the vine was a small pumpkin. Adam was shrieking at the puppy and chasing her, whether objecting to her behavior or egging her on, Cindy didn't know.

"Oh, Doggy, no!" She went into the yard, corraled the energetic pup and managed to take the pumpkin vine away from her. "Now look what you've done. You killed Luke's nice pumpkin plant."

"It was a volunteer, anyway," Luke said. "There used to be a garden back here, but I never paid attention to it."

"Maybe we can replant the vine." She knew absolutely nothing about gardens, but the vine, with its little pumpkin a long way from ripe, looked so sad she felt compelled to try to save it. She found the hole where Doggy had ripped it up, stuck the root ball back in the ground and scooped dirt around it.

"Hey, there are all kinds of vines back here," said Luke, poking at the weedy patch of ground with his foot. "More pumpkins, some gourds, acorn squash—I'm not sure what all these are. It's amazing they've survived with all these weeds.

"Not to mention, I've never watered back here."

Adam had taken an interest in the pumpkin replanting and was now patting at the dirt around the vine, trying to imitate his mother.

"That's right, Adam," Cindy said. "We leave these nice vines in the ground."

"I think I'll get a rake and clean this up. You like pumpkin pie, right?"

"Are you kidding? I make the best pumpkin pie in the county. I can do a lot with acorn squash, too. And I love fresh cantaloupe."

By silent agreement, they worked on the garden together. Cindy didn't know what she was doing, but she could tell the difference between a weed and a good plant, so she started yanking up anything that didn't look as if it might bear fruit or flower. Luke made another trip to the hardware store, returning with some metal edging, a couple of bags of dirt and some pansies in little pots.

It felt nice to dig in the warm dirt, Cindy discovered. Luke showed her how to plant pansies and she really got into the task. Luke followed her with a watering can.

"I did get over it, you know," he said, continuing the conversation that had been interrupted earlier as if they'd never paused. "I thought I was going to die when you said you didn't want to marry me."

"I wasn't all that pleased when you said you didn't want to travel with me. You said you thought it was just an impractical fantasy and that I would outgrow it."

"I don't remember saying that," he said. "But if you say I did, then it's probably true. I guess we remember what we want to remember. It seemed all one-sided to me—you refused to marry me and we broke up. Anyway, you did break my poor little teenage heart."

"You broke mine, too," she said quietly.

"But I did get over it. I haven't been pining silently for you all these years. But the things that drew us together then are still inside us. It only makes sense that now that you're free again and we're around each other I'd start to feel something for you again. I'm sorry if my timing is inconvenient."

He didn't really sound all that sorry, she thought. "I can't deny I'm finding it very hard to resist you. The things I once loved about you are still there. But the things that drove us apart are still there, too. I don't want to repeat history."

They stopped to admire their handiwork. It wasn't the most beautiful garden in the world. The plants were more or less random. But Cindy still felt a strange sense of accomplishment at turning chaos into order.

Even with things so unsettled between herself and Luke, she'd felt relaxed for the first time in a very, very long time. She had a job, which meant she would no longer have to beg for food and housing and other favors. But the job didn't start for a few days. Those days stretching out ahead of her gave her a heady sense of freedom.

No diner to worry about. No wedding to plan. She was moved in, settled.

She wanted to go someplace.

"Hey, Luke, would you mind if I took a little weekend trip?"

"Why would I mind?" he said, refusing to look at her.

"I thought I might join Sonya and Brenna and try to help them find Marvin."

Luke was already shaking his head. "I wasn't crazy about those two women striking out on their own, going after a criminal."

"Well, it's not like Marvin is violent or dangerous, except to women's peace of mind and their bank accounts."

"We don't know that."

"All the more reason they might need my help."

"You'll want to take Adam, I guess."

"Of course. He loves traveling in the car. And I won't put him in any danger."

"That's right, you won't. Not if I go with you to help protect him."

Chapter Ten

Cindy just stared at Luke for a few moments, her mouth hanging open. "You want to come with me?"

"I don't think you should go alone."

"I won't be alone. I'll be with Brenna and Sonya. And Adam, of course."

"Are you saying you'd rather I didn't come along?"

"Well, no, that's not what I'm saying." She looked uneasy. "It's just that in all the years I've known you I don't think you've traveled more than fifty miles from Cottonwood."

"I went away to college."

"All right, so I'm exaggerating. But if Texas

A&M had been in your backyard, you'd have been happier."

He had to admit she was right. Once he'd found a home here, he'd felt no desire to ever leave it. "Just because I haven't chosen to travel in the past doesn't mean I don't want to now."

She softened. "If it's something you really want to do, I'd love the company and someone to share the driving. And I guess it goes without saying that I have no money. I was going to ask you to lend me some, anyway. Now that I know I'll be able to pay it back, it doesn't feel so weird."

"It's not a problem. So, when do we leave?" He tried to inject some enthusiasm into his voice, though he felt no joy at the prospect of traveling. Except he'd be with Cindy and Adam, and that would make it tolerable.

"How about as soon as we can pack up the car?"

"Oh. What about Doggy?"

"We'll take her with us. Can we go in your Blazer? We'll have more room."

He imagined his car smelling like dog pee for the next year. "Sure. I'll go get packed."

He realized a few minutes later that he didn't have a suitcase. He must have put his clothes in *something* when he'd gone away to school, but he couldn't recall. So he put an extra pair of jeans and a few shirts in a big shopping bag, added the requisite underwear and socks. What else would he need?

Toothbrush. Razor. Shaving cream. Vitamins. Shampoo. A book to read, just in case. Soon he had another bag filled with necessities.

And what about food? They would get hungry driving. He raided his fridge and pantry for all his favorite snacks, in case they got stranded or couldn't find a restaurant. He remembered nothing of Louisiana from his childhood, but he understood it had some desolate areas. Pretty soon he had a cooler and a grocery sack full. Then there was Doggy. Had to bring her food, her dishes, her brush, a jug of water.

Cindy knocked at his kitchen door, and he paused long enough to let her in. "What's taking you so long?"

"Has it been that long?" he asked mildly, looking her over. She had a small backpack, a diaper bag and Adam.

She looked at the pile of stuff he'd accumulated for the trip. "All this for one weekend?"

"I like to be prepared."

"A radio? You're bringing a radio? Don't you have one in the car?"

"It's for the hotel room." He hated feeling

disconnected. If he didn't listen to the news on a regular basis, it made him uneasy.

"Most motels have TVs and radios. But I'll give you that. Now, this—" she picked up a two-pound barbell "—very essential."

"I don't like to miss my workouts. Hey, you've had more practice at this than me. I'm trying."

She smiled sheepishly. "Sorry. I shouldn't be razzing you. I know this isn't easy for you and I appreciate it."

"We can stop at a gas station on the way out of town and buy some maps."

"Oh, I don't need a map. I know where I'm going. I just talked to Sonya and Brenna. They're still in Smoky Bayou. They've found evidence that Marvin was there. Several people recognized his picture, though he's using a different name—Desmond Cox."

He didn't argue with her, but he was going to get a map, anyway. Leaving Cottonwood was bad enough. Not knowing exactly where he was would be torture. "I guess I'm ready." They loaded up the Blazer, and Luke double-checked that everything was locked, the curtains drawn, lights left on so it would look as if someone was home. He left a note for the neighbor asking her to pick up his newspaper and mail.

"Luke, we'll only be gone two days," Cindy pointed out for the third time.

"I just think it's a good idea to be prepared for any contingency."

They stopped at the gas station to fill up. Cindy noticed the stack of maps he'd bought, but she made no comment about them. Then they were off.

"Cottonwood city limits," Cindy announced as they left town. "Adam, wave bye-bye."

"Bye-bye!" Adam said excitedly.

"The apple doesn't fall far from the tree," Luke said with a smile. He tried to think of this as an exciting adventure. He was going for a romantic weekend getaway with the woman he was fast falling in love with. It was the perfect opportunity to woo her, to convince her they were right for one another. But with each mile he drove, he became more uneasy.

After about an hour, he couldn't stand it anymore. He pulled into a rest area.

"Why are we stopping?" Cindy asked.

"I want to check the map."

"We don't need to check the map. I know exactly where we are. I've driven this highway a hundred times."

"I need to check the map," he repeated, enunciating every word.

"Okay. Hey, why don't you let me drive? Then you can follow where we are on your map."

Now she was humoring him. Well, maybe he needed humoring. He wondered if Cindy was going to think he was an annoying travel companion. She gave Doggy and Adam both a brief outing before they set off again, Cindy behind the wheel, Luke with his finger on the map.

"The next town is Crocus," he announced. "In eight miles."

"Uh-huh. You know, you might try looking out the window. It's much more interesting than a map."

He forced himself to fold the map and enjoy the scenery. There wasn't much to look at except farmland interspersed with patches of pine forest.

"How long do you think it'll take to get to Smoky Bayou?" he asked.

"I imagine we won't get there before dark."

"Do you think the town has a motel?"

"Brenna and Sonya are staying at a bed-and-breakfast, but I don't think they take dogs."

"What will we do, then?"

"We'll find someplace. If not, we can sleep in the car."

"Oh, no. Not on your life. Maybe you can

curl up in a car seat and go to sleep, but I'm six foot two." Besides, his one consolation when he'd been taken away from his mother was that he wouldn't have to sleep in the car ever again. He hadn't, either. He'd endured a lot of unpleasant things, but that wasn't one of them.

"All right, don't get your shorts in a knot. We'll find a motel someplace. Oh, look! We're only twenty-two miles from the state line! A whole new state, Adam!"

Adam was fast asleep in his car seat, the puppy snoring next to him.

"I'll have to start a travel map for him. Jim and I each had a map. We colored in every new state we visited and put stars on the towns where we stayed overnight. We had national park passports, too. You know, where you get a stamp every time you visit a national park?"

Luke thought he should mind when Cindy talked about Jim. But it didn't really bother him, maybe because he knew Jim was gone. He couldn't bring himself to be jealous of a man who'd been taken so young, so cruelly and from such a terrific family. After all, it was Luke who was sitting here in this car with Cindy and Adam, living and breathing.

"Do you still have those things?" he asked gently.

"I guess I left them behind when I moved out of the house," she said. "I could start a new one for me, too. A new map for a new phase of my life."

"Had you been to all fifty states?"

"All but Hawaii."

"So do you need to see them again?"

She looked at him as if he was crazy. "Of course. Just because I've passed through Alabama a few times doesn't mean I've seen everything the state has to offer. As much as I've seen of this country, it's probably only a hundredth of one percent of what's out there to be discovered."

"And you want to discover it all."

"That's the thing. You can never discover it all. I've been to the Grand Canyon four times. But each time I see something completely different. They have ravens at the Grand Canyon. Did you know that?"

"No, I didn't."

"One time, I was sitting real still, and one flew up and landed about three feet from me. It was huge, the biggest darn bird I ever saw. It looked me right in the eye."

When Cindy talked about her travels and the wonders she'd seen, she got a different look on her face. Her eyes sparkled with excitement and awe. Even her voice sounded different—animated, like a little girl's.

Maybe he was wrong to want to take that from her, he thought with a twinge of guilt. But then he thought about Adam, and he strengthened his resolve. Children, especially babies, didn't crave adventure. Adam wasn't old enough to appreciate the historical significance of a Civil War battlefield or the grandeur of a snowy mountain peak. He needed familiar things, familiar people, a schedule to follow, regular and nutritious meals. True, he was an unusually adaptable baby, and he didn't complain much about anything, but that didn't mean that having his life in a constant uproar of change was good for him.

It certainly hadn't been healthy for Luke when he was little.

At Cindy's insistence, they stopped at a rustic-looking diner in a no-name town. Signs in the window advertised all-you-can-eat shrimp and Cajun dishes. Luke knew enough about Cajun food to predict that he wouldn't like it. He wasn't crazy about highly spiced food. But Cindy had rejected his suggestion that they stop at a popular family restaurant chain, which he knew would have a high chair for Adam and some good ole fried chicken for him.

"Haven't you eaten there," Cindy asked, "like, a bazillion times?"

"Not at this exact one," he countered.

She rolled her eyes. "You need to try new things every once in a while."

As if this whole trip wasn't something new for Luke. Still, he was determined not to be a stick-in-the-mud. So they went inside the Cajun restaurant, where a gum-popping waitress seated them at a long picnic table alongside some good ole boys.

Cindy ordered gumbo and a side of plain rice. Luke ordered the only thing on the menu that looked safe—a hamburger and French fries. He got a suspicious sideways look from a couple of their fellow diners.

"You ain't from around here, is you?" one of the guys asked in a tone that was hard to interpret. Friendly curiosity? Or accusation?

"We're from Cottonwood, Texas," Luke answered, which brought no warmth to the other man's eyes. So Luke added, for good measure, "I'm a deputy sheriff there."

Cindy kicked him under the table. "We're just passing through. Say, I think I know you," she said to the other man. "Don't you drive for Texaco sometimes?"

The man immediately warmed up. "Well, yes, I do. Where do I know you from?"

She stuck out her hand. "Cindy Lefler. My husband and I drove a green rig with an armadillo on the side."

The other man's face lit up with recognition. "Oh, yeah, I remember you. How is ole Jim?" And his eyes flashed suspiciously at Luke.

One of the other good old boys elbowed his friend. "Jim died, you idiot. Don't you remember?"

Somehow they got through the awkward moment. The waitress brought their food. Cindy mashed up some rice and beans and broth for Adam, but he wanted nothing to do with it.

"What's wrong, kiddo?" Cindy asked, concerned. "You love rice and beans."

"Maybe it's too hot for him," Luke suggested. "This food's pretty spicy."

"I've never found anything this kid won't at least try." He wouldn't try the bread pudding they got for dessert, either, which troubled Cindy even more.

It worried Luke a little, too. The bread pudding was the only part of the meal he really enjoyed. What kid turned down something sweet like that?

When they returned to the Blazer, Cindy

used Luke's cell phone to call home and see if she had any messages from Sonya and Brenna. She did. They'd called to say they'd finally found someone who knew where Marvin was, or at least where he'd been headed when he'd left Smoky Bayou. He'd met some girl who was the cousin of someone else, and she lived in another small town, Faring, about fifty miles away. The rumor was that Marvin, aka Desmond, had left with her.

"So Sonya and Brenna have left Smoky Bayou?" Luke asked, just to be sure he understood the situation.

Cindy nodded. "But I think we should stop there for the night, anyway. By the time we got to Faring, it would be too late to do anything. And I think Adam's tired. I don't like it that he wouldn't eat any dinner."

At least she was putting Adam first. Not that he believed Cindy would do anything else. "I'd rather stop, too," he agreed. "Then we can get an early start in the morning."

By the time they made it to Smoky Bayou, it was nine o'clock. Adam was uncharacteristically fussy. And Doggy, who'd been a surprisingly good traveler, had started whining incessantly.

They passed one motel on the way into town. "It doesn't look too bad," Cindy said.

Luke thought it looked awful, with its barely functioning neon light and garish paint. "Surely they have a Holiday Inn."

"You usually find those big chains near the interstate," Cindy said.

They drove all the way through town and didn't see any other choices. So they turned around and went back to the uncreatively named Bayou Inn. Luke secured two rooms for them which weren't as bad as he feared they might be. They were basic but clean, with cable TV and hot and cold running water. They even had a connecting door.

Luke helped Cindy carry in her few belongings while Adam howled out his displeasure. Unlike some mothers Luke had seen, Cindy had no ability to simply tune out a fussy child. She paced with him and jiggled and cajoled, offered him all different kinds of food choices, changed his diaper.

Doggy seemed distressed that her new best friend was unhappy. She watched with big, worried brown eyes.

"Do you want me to do anything?" Luke asked.

"I don't know. I've never seen him like this."

"Is he teething?"

"He doesn't act like that's the problem. Oh, Luke, I think he might be running a fever."

Luke felt the baby's forehead. He did feel warm and he looked a little flush. "Do you have any baby aspirin?"

"No. Adam's never been sick, not once, so I've never had to buy any. Do you think there's a drugstore around?"

"I didn't notice anything open. They roll up the sidewalks here at night, I think."

"Well, I've got to do something. This just isn't normal. Let's go ask the motel manager if there's a drugstore nearby. Surely there's some-place people around here can go late at night."

The manager, a very nice Bangladeshi man who spoke excellent English, told them the closest clinic or hospital was in Alexandria.

"But that's, like, a hundred miles away," Cindy said. "What about a drugstore?"

The man shook his head, looking at Adam with concern. "My wife was a doctor in our country. But she is not licensed to practice here."

Cindy's eyes lit up with hope. "It wouldn't hurt to have your wife just look at Adam, would it?"

"I will get her."

After a few minutes, Cindy, Luke and Adam

were shown back to the manager's living quarters, a small but neat one-bedroom apartment. Two thin, dark-haired children slept on the sofa, and Adam's squalling didn't even wake them up.

The manager's wife, whose name was Veda, was a tiny woman with thick, black hair bound in a loose braid down her back. Still in her nightgown and robe, she examined Adam on her kitchen table. She had a stethoscope and one of those gadgets doctors use to look into babies' ears. Her English was not quite as good as her husband's, but with the husband there to translate and clarify, it finally became clear that she believed Adam probably had a stomach bug of some kind, nothing serious.

"I will make some special tea," Veda said, and she began measuring and pouring various powders and liquids into a pot on the stove. "It will settle his stomach and bring down his fever."

"Are you sure that's safe?" Luke whispered in Cindy's ear.

"Is this a cure from your country?" Cindy asked.

"We've been using this for hundreds of years," the manager said. "Do not worry."

A buzzer called him to the front desk—someone else wanted to check in. He went to take care of it.

Veda poured the tea into an old peanut-butter jar. It was a strange black color. She told Cindy to let it cool, then give Adam about six ounces from a bottle.

Cindy thanked her profusely, and Luke tried to pay her, but she refused the money. "It's not allowed," she said firmly. She probably had a healthy fear of the AMA coming down on her for practicing medicine without a license.

"Maybe we should just drive to the hospital in Alexandria," Luke said as they crossed the parking lot back to their rooms.

"Nonsense. Veda is a mother herself. She's not going to give me anything that would poison my child. Don't be suspicious just because it's not what you're used to seeing."

Luke still felt uneasy as Cindy fed Adam the tea. But the baby drank it willingly, almost eagerly, as if he knew it was exactly what he needed. His crying quieted down almost immediately, and fifteen minutes later he was asking, in his own unique way, for food.

Cindy fed him some cereal and a little bit of fruit, and soon he was nodding off.

"He feels cooler," she said with obvious relief. She put him to bed in a portable crib Veda had loaned them. And when Doggy whined, Cindy put the puppy in with the baby.

"I'm glad it wasn't any worse," Luke said. "But, Cindy, have you really thought about what you would do if it *was* worse?"

She shrugged. "We'd have driven to Alexandria."

"Yeah, more than an hour away. A lot can happen, medically speaking, in an hour." He paced the small room, too nervous to sit next to Cindy on the bed—and too aware of her as a woman, looking all warm and maternal as she smoothed Adam's scant, silky hair off his forehead.

"What do you think the people who live here do?" she countered.

"We don't have that problem in Cottonwood."

"Of course we do. The hospital is forty-five miles away in Tyler."

"But we have Ed and Jeff Hardison. They'll still make house calls."

"And the people of Smoky Bayou have Veda. I'll bet Adam isn't the first baby she's doctored at her kitchen table."

"I'm just saying—"

"I know what you're saying. Out here traveling in the big, bad world, terrible things can happen. If disaster strikes, you have to rely on the kindness of strangers. I understand that, and I understand that it worries you sick. Traveling does involve some degree of risk. But it's calculated risk, and I believe the rewards are worth it."

"But this is your child we're talking about. How can you put *him* at risk just to satisfy your wanderlust?"

A fierce expression came over her face. "How dare you imply I'm being selfish. I would gladly lay down my life for this child, you know that. Dammit, Luke, you *know* that. But I can't wrap him in bunting and lock him inside the house just because I'm afraid he'll get hurt."

"I'm not suggesting that. But you can't think getting dragged all over the world is good for a child."

"Yes. I really do believe that. I want him to grow up knowing all kinds of people and places and cultures. I want him to grow up free of prejudice and with all kinds of experiences, so he'll have a broad knowledge base when it comes time for him to decide what he wants to do with his life. I don't want him to be like me, baking biscuits every day because my mother and grandmother baked biscuits every day.

"The people of Cottonwood—God love 'em, they're wonderful, good-hearted people, but most of them can't see past the noses on their faces. Most of them have never *seen* a Bangladeshi person, let alone given their child an exotic curative tea. But look at Adam now. He's at least as well off as he would have been had this happened at home. Maybe better."

Luke studied the sleeping child, who now had his arms wrapped around a sleeping, contented puppy, and he had to agree. It had all turned out well.

"I didn't mean to go on such a tear," Cindy said self-consciously. "It's just that, as many times as I've tried to explain it to you, you never seem to get it."

"You didn't travel much as a child, did you?" he said.

"No. We could never go anywhere because of the café."

"I did. Before I was six years old, I seldom slept in the same place two nights in a row. All I wanted was my own bed. A closet to hang my clothes in. Maybe a dog. What I usually got was the back seat of the car or a pallet on someone's floor.

"It wasn't fun, Cindy. Not at all."

Chapter Eleven

Cindy held her breath. When she and Luke had been kids, she'd tried and tried to get him to tell her about his early childhood, what his life had been like before he'd arrived at Polly's when he was fourteen. Sometimes he'd made stuff up to satisfy her—saying his parents had been killed while mountain climbing in the Alps. Or that his parents had been circus performers and he'd run away when they'd tried to make him Cannonball Boy.

She'd recognized the fantasies for what they were, of course, but she'd never succeeded in getting a serious answer out of Luke. The closest she'd ever come was when he'd said his childhood was not worth rehashing.

A couple of weeks ago, he'd dropped that little bombshell about how he'd been taken away from his mother. But then he'd clammed up.

Seeing him now, unguarded as his unhappy memories flickered across his face, she wasn't sure she wanted to know the truth. But she needed to know. She needed to understand why one town had become so important to him that it was a major undertaking to set foot outside the city limits.

"Tell me, Luke," she said softly. She gently shifted Adam to one side of the bed, then scooted over herself to make room so Luke could sit next to her. "Come on, sit down. I'm tired of you pacing like a caged tiger."

He yanked off his shoes and sat on the bed, carefully positioning himself so he was close but not touching her.

"I never knew my father," Luke said. "I'm not sure my mother even knew who he was. She was an alcoholic and a drug addict."

Cindy's heart squeezed in on itself. It was hard to imagine Luke, so big and solid and wholesome now, being born to such circumstances.

"We lived in our car most of the time, an old,

green Country Squire station wagon. Sometimes my mom would work, but most of the time she didn't. She floated from boyfriend to boyfriend—or, if she was between men, from one disgusted relative to the next. If anyone ever gave her anything, she sold it for drugs. If they tried to be kind to her, take her in, she stole from them."

Cindy's hand crept up to cover her mouth so she wouldn't make any outbursts of horror. She didn't want to say or do anything to stop the narrative.

"But I will say one thing for her. She loved me. She wanted to be a good mother, but she just didn't know how."

"How can you—" She stopped herself. She hadn't been there, didn't know Luke's mother. She had no right to judge.

"If there was food available, she always fed me first. The one time I remember getting sick, she did manage to get me to a doctor. And she never, ever let anyone hurt me. One of her boyfriends tried, once. She left him just like that, though we had nowhere to go and not a dime to our name."

"What happened to her?" Cindy asked, fearing the worst.

"Child Protective Services finally caught up

with her. They took me away, put me in foster care, told me she had to get clean before she could have me back."

"Did she?" Cindy asked, already knowing the answer.

Luke shook his head. "I never saw her again. And I don't think it was because she didn't want me. They just wouldn't let her have contact with me. Even if she'd wanted to get off drugs and booze, she didn't have the slightest idea how to do it and no one to turn to. She'd alienated everyone who ever cared about her by then."

Oh, Lord. No wonder Luke had gone to such lengths to keep Beverly Hicks from taking Adam away. But that brought up a troubling thought. Did Luke equate her with his drug-addicted mother? Was he trying to be that person his mom never had, the one who would have helped her see the light, reform her, make her a better parent?

She supposed she couldn't blame him for focusing on her shortcomings. She had, after all, tried to live on a boat.

She put her arms around him and leaned her head on his shoulder. "I'm so sorry, Luke. I wish you'd explained this to me a long time ago."

"It's not something I think about often. I got past it and moved on."

Clearly there was still some baggage, but she didn't want to argue with him. After all, he had overcome devastating odds to become the man he was now. "Oh, Luke, you grew up to be a good, good man." A rush of affection for him welled up inside her. She couldn't even express what she felt. Gratitude, certainly, as well as admiration for his high ideals and his belief in his own principles. But she felt something else, as well, something she couldn't put a name to. It wasn't an emotion so much as a need, and it wasn't a sexual need so much as a desire to connect with all that was good and whole in Luke. She wanted to nurture the flowers that bloomed in the garden of his soul despite the ugly, choking weeds of his childhood that had tried to snuff out his spirit.

She touched his face, coaxed him to look at her. She saw an answering need in his eyes, but hesitation, too. She shouldn't be too surprised. She'd put that hesitation there. Just hours ago she'd told him she didn't want to start anything.

She had changed her mind.

"I think I'd like to finish that kiss now," she said, the request coming out a husky whisper.

He looked at her with surprise at first, then a rueful smile. "Cindy, honey, we are on a bed in a cheap motel. If I kiss you here, it's going to put all kinds of ideas in my head."

The same ideas that were already swimming around in hers. But he was right. They shouldn't. He hadn't come with her on this trip for romantic reasons but for protection and moral support. But if she didn't remove herself physically from him, she wasn't going to be responsible for her actions. Why did he have to smell so good? Why did that scratchy day-old beard of his suddenly seem so sexy?

"Maybe we better say good night, then." She reluctantly pulled away from him. "We have to get up early tomorrow."

"Right." Suddenly he was all business. He scooted off the bed, bent down to pick up his running shoes. "I'll just go to my room, then."

She stood up and walked him to the connecting door, knowing she should push him through it, then close it and lock it. He was just too much damn temptation looking all rumpled, with his long-sleeved T-shirt half untucked, his dark hair tousled.

"We can leave the door open a crack," he said. "That way I can hear you if you have any more trouble with Adam."

"Good idea."

They lingered in the doorway, not looking at each other as hard as they could. Finally Luke said, "If you didn't bring birth control with you, we're both in trouble." He didn't give her any chance to answer—he hauled her against his chest and kissed her.

This was much different than this morning's polite, gentle kiss. This was the kiss of a man claiming his woman. He backed her up against the door frame, cushioning her head from the hard metal with one hand while holding her wrist prisoner with the other. It was like a submission hold he might put on a reluctant prisoner. Except she was anything but reluctant.

She kissed him back with a mindlessness that frightened her. A small part of her reminded her this wasn't wise. She might have a greater understanding of Luke, more empathy, but they still had the same fundamental differences they'd had an hour ago, and all the understanding in the world wasn't going to change that.

But right then she just couldn't bring herself to care about their differences—except those very intriguing physical ones.

His assault on her senses slowed and gentled slightly. Oh, heaven help her, if he changed his mind now, she would burst into tears of frustration.

"Birth control," he whispered in her ear. "I'm crazy to have you, but I sure as hell didn't bring anything."

She nibbled on his earlobe. "You weren't expecting a romantic tryst?"

He groaned and his knees almost buckled. "You know that drives me insane. Don't do it unless you have a condom in your suitcase."

"No condom. But we don't need one."

He forced himself to look into her eyes. "We don't?"

"I'm safe."

Apparently that was a good enough answer, because he resumed his kisses. She was tense with excitement, expecting him to grab her at any moment, carry her to his bed and start ripping her clothes off. That was how it had been for them as teenagers. Though it had taken years for them to get to that point, once they'd crossed the line, it was as if they'd opened Pandora's box. They couldn't get enough sex, and they could never get it fast enough.

Now, however, Luke trailed a line of kisses across her jaw and down her neck, then slowly unfastened just two buttons of her lightweight sweater. He dipped his tongue between her breasts, and she almost lost it right there.

So, Luke had learned a few refinements over the past ten years.

"Do that again," she whispered.

He did. Then he undid two more buttons, careful not to tear the delicate sweater's fabric. She could remember instances when shirt buttons had gone flying, and she'd had to buy a needle and thread at the drugstore and repair her clothes before she could go home.

He unhooked the front clasp of her bra, taking both breasts in his hands as if testing their weight.

Her breathing came faster and her head was almost spinning. "Luke, please, I'm going to fall down if we don't move to the bed."

Then he did scoop her up and carry her all of about five feet to his bed. He'd already turned down the spread. Now he shoved blankets and sheets and pillows out of his way, as if clearing a space for some grand artistic effort.

She laughed in giddy delight as her body remembered things her mind had forgotten— what it felt like to feverishly peel off snug jeans, the soft texture of the light dusting of hair on Luke's chest, that washboard stomach.

She kept getting distracted as she tried to

remove his clothes, wanting to taste his skin here and there. His skin tasted the way she remembered, the sensory input thrusting her back in time to when sex was forbidden, a little bit scary and better than it had ever been since.

Dex had been a skilled lover. Not a passionate one, though. Why hadn't she seen that? What he did was paint-by-numbers when compared to Luke's earthy, spontaneous actions.

He loosed her hair from its ponytail and rubbed his face in it. "You still use the same shampoo."

"Lavender scent. But not all of me is the same." She'd not completely lost all the weight she'd gained during her pregnancy.

Luke ran one hand along her slightly rounded stomach, then back up to her breasts. "Motherhood has agreed with you."

"You're kind to say so."

"No, really. You still look like you, but sexier."

She was relieved he didn't expect her pert teenage body. "And you still look like you, but with a few more muscles." She tested one of those muscles now, his biceps. It was hard as granite. The sheer power of his grown-up body thrilled her, reminding her that they weren't the same two kids who had thrashed in back seats.

They had all these years of living to bring to their lovemaking. Luke had learned to be tender as well as passionate. And she had learned to be patient, to enjoy the journey as well as the destination.

She was really enjoying this journey, she thought hazily as Luke kissed her nipples and ran gentle fingers through the curls that guarded her femininity, feathering close to but not quite touching the place she wanted him to touch.

She wondered fleetingly what woman had taught him how to tease, then dismissed the thought. She didn't really want to know.

Luke lay back on the sheet beside her and pulled her against him for another series of steamy kisses. She threw her leg over him, registering the feel of his arousal against her thigh, imagining how it would be when he finally entered her. Her juices flowed more freely at the thought. She was so hot, so darn wanton.

She no longer thought about what was happening, her brain short-circuited. She let her instincts guide her, following one incredible sensation to the next, rolling on top of Luke, then letting him take the dominant position, until they were both completely crazed.

Now *this* was what she remembered. He

pulled her legs apart and plunged inside, all in one fluid movement, and she cried out at the joy she felt in their physical reunion.

Her eyes formed tears of emotions ratcheted up so high she couldn't contain them. She called out his name again and again as he thrust ever more deeply inside her. He was no doubt as mindless as she was at this point.

Yet he sensed when she was close to her climax. He shifted his angle, moved faster, harder, all without any prompting from her. And, yes, that was it, she was there. Her stomach swooped and her world exploded into thousands of fiery arrows of sensation all landing in one bull's-eye.

Even in the midst of her incredible crescendo, she knew when he reached his own peak, just moments after she did. His whole body went tense and then, with one final, magnificent thrust, he emptied himself into her, crying out her name.

They both collapsed against the damp sheets, thoroughly spent. Cindy reclaimed enough of her senses to listen for Adam, in case their crazed vocalizations had awakened him. But he remained quiet.

Thank heavens he was a sound sleeper.

"Was it like you remembered?" Luke asked

after several soft, silent minutes of reveling in afterglow.

"Yes and no. For one, we aren't madly searching for clothes, trying to get dressed in a cramped back seat so I can get home before curfew."

Luke laughed softly. "I like this better. I always wanted to hold you like this. I always wanted to sleep with you, to wake up next to you. In a real bed."

That was a nice thought. A not-so-nice thought was what would happen after they woke up tomorrow morning. But she pushed it from her mind. She wasn't a worrier by nature. She much preferred living in the moment, though that tendency had often gotten her into trouble.

Luke, once again proving how different he was from her, immediately took up worrying. "Are you sure you won't get pregnant? Not that that would be the worst thing in the world…"

She didn't really want to explain this part to him. She was embarrassed by her decision now. But she didn't want to mislead him. "I can't have any more babies."

Silence.

"I'm sure you want to know why, so I'll tell you. When Adam was born, I had my tubes tied."

"Why?" The question was innocent enough, but she could feel the sudden tension in his body.

"If I tell you, you'll think I'm an awful person."

"I could never think that, Cindy."

Oh, yes, he could. But she supposed he deserved to know. If he had any fantasies about happily ever after for them, he needed to know this one thing about her.

"I got pregnant with Adam by accident. And frankly I wasn't too happy about it. I liked my life just fine. Jim and I had no ties to anything, no responsibilities beyond paying the insurance on our truck and delivering the next payload on time. I knew a child would change everything.

"But Jim was thrilled, and he reassured me that everything would be okay, that we would adapt. And he talked me into buying a house and settling down."

Luke said nothing, but she knew what he was thinking. *Jim was a smart man.* Though Jim and Luke were very different, they agreed on one point—children should have a stable home, a town and a community to call their own.

"I was terrified at the prospect of becoming a mother," she continued. "I was positive I would be very bad at it, and I felt guilty for getting pregnant when I really didn't want children. On top of that, my pregnancy was incredibly difficult."

"I remember you didn't work at the diner very much when you were pregnant."

"I had all sorts of health problems, including diabetes and hypertension. I was restricted to bed the last month, and I swear I almost lost my mind. So I talked it over with Jim. I said I would try really hard to be a good mother. But I didn't want any more children."

"And he agreed?"

"Yes. Toward the end of my pregnancy he was really worried something would happen to me. So we signed the papers."

Luke said nothing.

"It turned out being a mother was the most natural thing I ever tried to do. And almost immediately I realized I'd acted rashly. But, hey, I was a hormone-riddled, crazy pregnant woman when I signed the consent forms. In retrospect, it wasn't the best time to make a decision like that. But I did and it's done and I have to live with it. Adam will be my only child."

Luke remained silent.

"C'mon, Luke, say something. If you think I'm some grotesque aberration of womanhood, better tell me now."

"Nothing like that."

"Then what?"

He shook his head, laughing at his own foolishness. "Way back when, when I asked you to marry me, I had a fantasy about a home and a white picket fence—and children. I wanted to have children with you." He turned onto his side and propped his head on his hand. "I've never entirely lost the fantasy."

"So you shouldn't even waste your time with me," she murmured.

"Cindy." He kissed her nose. "What I've realized is that the world is already full of children. I don't need to make more in some misguided attempt to atone for the damage done to me."

She was more relieved to hear that than she should have been. If he would just reject her here and now for her lapse in maternal yearnings, it would be much easier to let go of any notion that she and Luke should get back together.

"So you don't regret what just happened?" she asked, actually holding her breath anticipating his answer.

"It didn't just happen. We made it happen. And no, I don't regret it. Ever since Jim died, I've let myself think about what it might be like to… Well, I might as well admit it. I had plans.

But I planned to wait a decent interval, to let you grieve. Then came Dexter Shalimar..."

"No wonder you disliked him so much. Oh, Luke, I wish I'd listened to you. I feel so stupid."

"Don't keep beating yourself up over that." He pulled her against him, snuggling more deeply into the mushy mattress. Normally he hated soft mattresses, but this one felt more like a nest the way it caused them to fall into each other. "Anyway, even if you'd sent Marvin packing, that didn't mean you would have wanted me."

"It's not a question of wanting. Oh, Luke, you must know I want you."

"But there are other things you want more."

"There's something that's part of me, something I was born with, some kind of restlessness. I can't ignore it or deny it. If I could cut it out with a knife, or take some kind of pill to get rid of it..." She stopped herself before she told a lie. Life would be much simpler if she could be a homebody. But she honestly believed that her yearning for adventure was a good thing. If more people were less afraid of change, less threatened by people and ideas that were different than their own, the world would be a better place.

"No, you wouldn't want to get rid of it."

"Not only do I want to keep it," she admitted, "I want Adam to experience it, as well. And I wouldn't want you to change your nature, either. You're so much a part of Cottonwood, you might as well have been born there. I can't imagine the town without you."

"Which leaves us at a stalemate," he said glumly.

Chapter Twelve

They spoke no more of their past or future that night. They got up long enough to brush their teeth and take Doggy out for one last potty break. Luke was worried that Cindy would retreat to her own room, but she didn't. They came back to Luke's bed, held each other throughout the night, woke early and made love again. It was so pleasurable, it didn't even feel real to Luke, more like a fragile spiderweb of a fantasy. The more they talked of the past or the future, the more those thin strands of web were strained.

So they didn't. Perhaps Cindy believed they had this moment together and that was all. He refused to think that way.

Adam seemed back to his usual happy, healthy self in the morning. They ate breakfast at the diner next door to the motel, and Adam crammed eggs into his mouth with his bare hands despite Cindy's attempts to feed him with a spoon.

"Oh, Adam, yuck!" she objected after wiping off his hands and face for the third time. But she was laughing, clearly relieved that he was back to being her happy, rambunctious little boy.

They met up with Sonya and Brenna later that morning, at a city park in Faring, Louisiana.

The two women greeted Cindy as if she were their long-lost sister, and Luke realized that their shared victimization had bonded the three women as closely as blood might have in other circumstances. They seemed to share a silent understanding that he wasn't a party to.

"So, what have you found out?" Luke asked, wanting to get down to business.

"He's definitely been here," Sonya said. "People remember him and the car. They said he took up with a bank teller named Shelly. She lives in that house over there." Sonya pointed to a tidy brick bungalow across the street and down half a block. "That's why we're here.

No one answers the door and no one seems to know where she might have gone. But her car is in the garage."

"We're gonna wait 'til she comes home, then question her," Brenna said. "And if the jerk's with her, we'll grab him."

"Now, wait a minute," Luke cautioned. "You can't go taking the law into your own hands."

"Then *you* arrest him," Brenna said belligerently.

"I can't. This is out of my jurisdiction. But I can see if the local law will help us out."

Brenna folded her arms. "Don't hold your breath. We already talked with the local sheriff here. He's a redneck good ole boy who as good as told me we were hysterical females who were imagining things."

Women with vengeance on their minds were dangerous creatures. Not that he wanted to be labeled as sexist as the local sheriff, but he'd seen the damage a scorned woman could do, and it wasn't pretty.

He needed to convince these women—intelligent women, all three—not to do anything rash. "So, what's your plan?"

"As soon as we spot him," Sonya said, sounding like the voice of reason, "we're going to confront him. That's all."

"And if he pretends he's never seen you before?" Luke figured that was exactly what would happen. "Are you going to jump him, hog-tie him, drag him back to Dallas or Houston? The moment you lay a hand on him, he'll have *you* arrested—for assault."

"I'd gladly go to jail," Brenna said, "as long as he's locked up, too."

"Oh, you would not," Sonya argued. "Deputy Rheems is right. We've done well with our detective work. Let's not blow it now and scare him into hiding."

"I'll go talk to the sheriff," Luke said.

Cindy handed Adam to Luke. "Here, take Adam."

"I'm happy to take Adam," he said affably. "But do you think the sheriff will take me seriously with a baby in my arms?"

"I just want him out of harm's way—in case Marvin shows up while you're gone."

"Now, Cindy, promise me you won't confront—"

"I'm not promising you anything."

"You don't know what Marvin might be like if he's cornered."

"Just go talk to the sheriff," Cindy said. "I'm sure nothing will happen while you're gone."

* * *

"So, what's going on with you and the deputy?" Sonya asked innocently as she took a sip of coffee from a foam cup. She wore a lightweight, green silk pantsuit and delicate, high-heeled sandals—perfectly unsuited for a stakeout.

"Why do you think anything's going on?" Cindy asked, the picture of innocence.

Brenna burst out laughing, setting her wealth of silver jewelry to tinkling like wind chimes. "Oh, honey, I knew that man had it bad for you from the moment I saw you in the same room. But this morning he has a very different look to him."

"Yeah," Sonya agreed. "Kind of self-satisfied."

"Proprietary," Brenna added. "And he looks darn cute with a baby in his arms. There's just something about a big, strong lawman with a baby."

Cindy didn't see much use in lying about it. Besides, she would probably never see these women again. "Is it that obvious?"

The other women just smiled knowingly.

"Well, shoot."

"I don't know what you're complaining about," Sonya said.

Cindy rolled an acorn around with her foot. "It's complicated."

"Isn't it always?" Brenna commented. "So what's wrong?"

Cindy stretched her legs out on the picnic bench. She wasn't used to sitting and doing nothing, unless she counted the week she'd spent moping after she learned she'd been jilted and financially ruined. "We dated in high school."

"Ah, a past." Brenna leaned forward. "Did you do the dirty?" She gasped. "He was your first, I'll bet."

Cindy could feel her face flaming.

Sonya cleared her throat. "Don't embarrass the poor girl. She's entitled to *some* privacy."

"Uh-uh, not while there's a juicy story waiting to be told. So, what happened?"

"I like to travel," Cindy said. "Luke doesn't even own a suitcase. For this weekend, he packed his clothes in a brown grocery sack."

"Oh, that's sad." Brenna finished her coffee and wadded up the cup. "So, that's it? That's the big problem that's kept you apart for, like, ten years?"

"Well, I got married to someone else, too."

Brenna's eyes—a bright, grass green—widened with interest. "What happened there?"

Sonya frowned disapprovingly. "Brenna, down, girl."

"No, it's okay," Cindy said with a laugh. She

found Brenna's open curiosity refreshing. At least she was honest. She reminded Cindy of Doggy, who was currently winding her leash about the picnic table legs, getting hopelessly tangled as she snuffled for discarded scraps. "My husband died and left me a big insurance benefit. That's why I was such an attractive target for Marvin."

Brenna was immediately contrite. "Oh, gosh, Cindy, I'm sorry. Me and my big mouth."

"No, it's really okay. I've come to terms with it. Jim lived a short life, but it was very full."

"So, back to the deputy," Brenna said, fishing around in her huge backpack until she found what she wanted—a package of Twinkies. Sonya winced when she saw them but said nothing. "You say he doesn't like to travel, but obviously he overcame his distaste long enough to come here with you."

"These are special circumstances. And, believe me, he's not enjoying it."

"Not enjoying it?" Brenna laughed again, throwing her head back.

"He's not," Cindy insisted. "I want to travel the world. I don't want my son to grow up like me, stuck in a one-horse town where everything is always the same. I want him to have culture and history. I want him to have friends all over the globe. I want him to have choices. I mean, you girls know what I'm talking about. You both live in the city, where there's diversity and museums and...and Indian food. I bet you couldn't find a speck of curry anywhere in Cottonwood. And I bet you've both traveled extensively."

Both women nodded. "I traveled a lot with my mother when I was growing up," Sonya said. "But I can't say it was much fun for me. We always stayed in four-star hotels and we hung out with other Americans just like us and we went on guided tours to all the tourist-trap places."

"I was a museum freak in college," said Brenna. "I went to any city, any country, that had a museum or gallery with jewelry or metalworking of any kind. But I always packed my suitcase with food instead of clothes. The thought of going without Twinkies and Wonder Bread is terrifying to me."

"So you weren't really interested in the travel, just the stuff in the glass cases," Cindy concluded.

"Pretty much. I was always happy to get home, sleep in my own bed. Then I would hole up in my studio for days on end and try to recreate what I'd seen."

"So I guess I'm the freak," Cindy said glumly. "I'm never happy to stay in one place. Marvin saw that need in me. And he capitalized on it. All he talked about was how much he had to travel for his business and how happy he would be to have a willing companion."

"You're not a freak," Sonya said diplomatically. "You're lucky in that you know what you want. And as for the deputy, he knows what he wants, too. There's a solution to this problem somewhere. You just have to think outside the box. You know, find a creative compromise."

"He thinks I'm a terrible mother for wanting to drag my child around and live out of a suitcase, because that's what his mother did to him when he was little. I just don't see how we could come to terms."

"Oh, my God," Sonya said suddenly. "Look."

Brenna and Cindy looked where Sonya pointed at the brick house. The front door was open. A pretty, young woman with long blond hair was peering outside, looking cautiously down the street in one direction, then the other.

Brenna casually picked up a pair of binoculars and looked through them. "She looks young."

"Oh, the poor thing," said Sonya.

The woman darted onto her porch and down the walkway in her bathrobe, snagged the newspaper and darted back inside.

"Bingo," Brenna said. "He's in there with her. I know he is. I say we go get him." She stood up, her hands bunched into fists.

"We should wait for Luke to get back," Cindy said reasonably, though she felt her blood boiling at the realization that Marvin was so close. Her money might be in the bank right here in this town—or more likely in cash squirreled away someplace where the IRS couldn't locate it.

"If we wait," Sonya said, "he might get away."

"Let's just move in closer to the house, so we'll be ready if he tries to leave," Brenna suggested. "He's definitely heard by now that two irate blondes are looking for him. He might be getting ready to bug out."

Sonya looked at Cindy. "You could wait here for Luke while we go on ahead."

That would be the reasonable thing to do. But suddenly Cindy wasn't feeling reasonable or sensible or willing to wait anywhere for anything. "I'll go with you. Luke won't have any trouble finding us." She untangled Doggy's leash and then they all walked up the sidewalk toward the bungalow.

"Let's not look so obvious," said Sonya. "We should amble, you know, like we're just out for a Saturday-morning stroll."

Brenna snorted. "No way people won't notice us. We're three blond strangers in a small town. I say let's just surround the house and yell catcalls until he comes out."

"No, no, no," Cindy argued. "I don't want to provoke him. We don't have any way to restrain him."

"My boot up his butt will restrain him," Brenna said, which made Cindy laugh despite the situation.

As they neared the small house, they paused with indecision.

"How about we cut through the yard next door and come around to the back?" Cindy suggested. "We're less likely to be seen. Maybe we can look in a window and know for sure whether he's there or not."

"Now that's a good idea," Brenna said. The house next door, separated from Shelly's house by a hedgerow, had no fences or gates. They simply cut through the yard to a dirt alley.

In back, Shelly's house was overgrown with lilac bushes.

"This is perfect," Cindy said. "And look, the window shade is open a few inches. We can sneak up and look right in."

"I'm not crawling through any bushes," Sonya huffed. Cindy could see she wasn't the crawling-through-bushes type, with her coordinated silk pantsuit, spike-heeled sandals and long, manicured nails.

"You keep watch, then," said Brenna, sounding impatient. "Whistle if you see someone coming."

"I don't know how to whistle."

"Yell, then. Do you have to take me so literally? Here, you watch the dog."

"Oh, I don't think—"

Brenna took Doggy's leash from Cindy and pressed it into Sonya's hand. The pup immediately jumped up on Sonya, placing a muddy paw right on her silk-clad knee.

"No!" Sonya and Cindy yelled together, causing Brenna to wince and put her hands over her ears.

"Chrissakes, you want to get us arrested for trespassing? Come on, Cindy." With that, Brenna dived behind the nearest lilac bush, crawling on her hands and knees between the shrubs and the taller hedgerow next door. Her heart thumping furiously, Cindy followed. She was pretty sure they couldn't be seen. Twigs and small branches slapped at her face as Brenna plunged ahead, letting them whip behind her.

"Ouch!" Cindy complained. "Hey, watch it."

"Shh! Okay, I can see the window from here. I'm just going to dart out, climb up on that air-conditioning unit and peek in the window."

"I'm coming, too."

They checked to make sure the coast was clear. Then they duckwalked out from under their cover until they reached the humming AC unit. The noise of the unit would mask any sounds they made.

Brenna climbed agilely onto the unit and leaned in toward the brick wall. But she was a tiny thing and she couldn't quite see in through the high window.

"Let me try," Cindy called out in a loud whisper. "I'm taller."

"All right," Brenna grumbled, clamoring down. "Sometimes it's a real drag being short."

Cindy's hands were clammy as she hoisted herself up on the AC unit. But even with her added height, she couldn't see in. If she could just get her feet a little closer to the wall... She tested the strength of a hose that ran from the AC to the house.

"Cindy," Brenna hissed, "that's not going to hold you."

"Yes, it is. I don't weigh much." She eased her weight onto the hose. It strained, but it didn't break. With her feet closer to the wall, she could stretch up and grab onto the outer windowsill. She had a perfect view inside.

"What do you see?" Brenna demanded anxiously.

"Oh, my God."

"Is it him?"

"Yes. He's in bed." He was stretched out, obviously naked, beneath an eyelet comforter in a frilly, feminine bedroom. It was, oh, so tempting to beat on the window, to let him know he'd been caught. The nerve, the absolute gall of that man made her cross-eyed with fury.

The bedroom door opened abruptly, and the young blond woman walked in with a heavily laden breakfast tray. She took one look at Cindy peering through the window and dropped the tray, screaming like a banshee.

Just then the hose gave way and Cindy plunged to the ground with a scream of her own and a very loud racket.

"Oh, my God!" Brenna came out of the bushes to help Cindy to her feet. "Are you okay?"

"I'm fine. Let's get out of here!"

"No, wait! He knows we're here now. What if he gets in Shelly's car and runs? We'd never catch him!"

It was a horrible possibility to be this close and have him get away. Cindy turned toward the house. "Marvin Carter!" she yelled. "Don't you go anywhere! The sheriff is on his way to arrest you! And if you try to run—" she couldn't think of what might happen if he ran, so she ended with "—he'll shoot you!"

By now Sonya had heard the commotion and come running. "What are you two idiots *doing?*"

Brenna grabbed the hands of the other two women. "I think we should get out of here before someone shoots us. People in Louisiana like their guns, you know."

"Which way?" Sonya asked.

"To the street, back to the park," said Cindy, knowing she would feel safer if they were near a car. "Maybe we really can get the sheriff to come now that we've found Marvin."

They cut through the lilacs and the hedgerow to the yard of the house next door, then ran full throttle toward the street. When they reached the sidewalk, however, Brenna skidded to a stop, nearly yanking Cindy and Sonya off their feet.

"Would you look at that," Brenna said in an awestruck voice.

Cindy looked, but she could hardly believe what she saw. Marvin Carter, her former phony fiancé, had just emerged from his new girlfriend's house *buck naked* and was running down the street away from them.

"Now that is just something you don't see every day," said Sonya.

Cindy was not about to let him get away. "Come on, girls, after him." And she took off running. She heard the thump of Brenna's boots and the clatter of Sonya's sandals behind her, but in her athletic shoes she was faster. As she saw Marvin running down Main Street in his birthday suit, she saw her future—and Adam's—running with him. He'd taken all of her savings, her parents' savings, Jim's life-insurance benefit, the money from the restaurant. All told, it was probably close to a million dollars.

Fury pumped adrenaline through her system, and she ran faster. Where was he going? How far could he get with no clothes? Townspeople out doing their morning errands stopped to point, shout or just stare at the spectacle. Cars stopped in the middle of the street.

Marvin turned and looked over his shoulder, and she saw the briefest instance of surprise on his face.

"Yeah, it's me!" she hollered. "I'm gonna kick your butt!"

He poured it on, putting some distance between them. Then he ducked down a side street.

Cindy turned the corner seconds later, but she saw no sign of him. Frustration welled up. He couldn't get away, he just couldn't! But it was as if he'd vanished.

She heard a car engine start up. That was it! He must have stashed a getaway vehicle somewhere in town just in case he had to make a sudden departure. Sure enough, the yellow Porsche came screeching out of an alley. She all but jumped on the car to stop it as it careened past her, but she had to settle for slapping her hand against the trunk as it got away.

Brenna sprinted around the corner, huffing and puffing, her face red. "He got away?"

Cindy could hardly talk, she was so winded. For a few moments she just stood there, bent over, pressing at the stitch in her side. "He had his car hidden. I guess he knew we were looking for him. What happened to Sonya?"

"Between her silly shoes and your silly dog, she couldn't keep up. Man, you're a fast runner."

"I'm not…really. I was just…highly motivated."

They put their arms around each other. Cindy wanted to cry.

"Guess maybe we shouldn't have spooked him," Brenna said.

Cindy didn't even want to think about what Luke would have to say on that subject.

Sheriff Wynn Tucker wasn't such a bad guy, Luke decided after a few minutes' conversation with the man. True, he hadn't taken Brenna and Sonya seriously. But Luke's credentials had impressed him enough that he'd listened to the story.

"We need to stop this man before he wipes out the finances of any more women," Luke said. "I don't need to tell you how dangerous it is that he's romancing a bank teller."

"Aw, now, Shelly's a good kid," Sheriff Tucker said, cleaning his aviator sunglasses with a handkerchief. "She wouldn't go in for no shenanigans."

"Not willingly. But I'm telling you this guy is good. He could trick her into giving him all kinds of information—people's account numbers, Social Security numbers. Not to mention the cash."

"So what do you reckon we should do about it?"

"He's wanted by the FBI," Luke said. "They haven't spent much energy looking for him, but I imagine if we could deliver him, they'd take him."

"The closest FBI office is in New Orleans," Tucker said. "I'll notify them, see how they want us to proceed."

"Good. Here's my cell phone number." Luke placed a card on Tucker's desk. "I think I should go back and keep an eye on Shelly's house, in case he returns—" Luke stopped. Had he just seen what he thought he'd seen?

Tucker was staring out the window, too. "Was that a naked man running down Main Street?" he asked, deadpan.

"I believe it was." And that was Cindy chasing him.

Both lawmen headed for the exit. Luke had a bad feeling about this.

Chapter Thirteen

"We could have had him," Luke said for at least the third time. Sharing coffee at the local diner with three attractive blondes should have been more fun than this, he reflected grimly.

"You don't have to keep saying that." Cindy poured some milk into a Tommy Tippee cup for Adam, then added the last bit to her own coffee, turning it to a milky beige.

"Luke's right," said Sonya. "We did something really stupid."

"It didn't seem stupid at the time," Brenna objected. "We were just trying to verify if he was in the house."

"Well, a naked man driving a yellow Porsche

shouldn't be all that hard to spot. The state police are on the lookout for him. Maybe we'll get lucky."

"What about his girlfriend?" Sonya asked.

"Yeah, what about her?" Cindy echoed.

Luke, along with Sheriff Tucker, had spent the past hour interrogating Shelly Bernard. In the end, though, they got nothing useful out of her. "She's claiming complete ignorance. Had no idea Marvin, aka Desmond Cox, wasn't the computer wizard he was claiming to be."

"Computer wizard?" Brenna laughed. "Where'd he come up with that one?"

"It sounds like his game was to target a low-tech bank," Luke continued, "then pretend to want to sell them a new automated system for a ridiculously low price."

"He could have worked that con all kinds of different ways," Cindy commented, picking at the tuna salad she'd ordered for lunch. "He could have actually gotten the bank to pay him for this nonexistent new system. Or he might have gotten direct access to bank accounts as he wormed his way into the confidence of the manager."

"Then there were the female employees themselves," Sonya said. "Any particular reason he picked this Shelly?"

"Her father owns the bank. She's got some money."

"And she's blond," said Cindy. "He obviously likes blondes."

"It's understandable," Luke said, his irritation ebbing as he looked at Cindy and felt the disappointment radiating from her. He tucked a strand of her hair behind her ear, the gesture automatic, ferreted out from some long-dormant memory bank.

Rather than shy away from his gesture, as he half expected her to, she seemed to lean into it. The look she shot his way was pure heat.

Brenna and Sonya watched the small intimacy with avid interest. He figured they knew what was going on, the way women always knew. They probably knew more than he did.

All of a sudden, Cindy started laughing. "He looked like an absolute idiot running down Main Street naked as a jaybird."

Soon Brenna joined her. "We must have scared him spitless, yelling at him from the backyard like that." Soon both women were laughing so hard, tears streamed down their faces.

Sonya watched, disapprovingly at first. But then her mouth started to twitch. "He must have been desperate to discard his dignity like that. And poor Shelly."

"You…you should have seen her face…when she saw me looking in the window," Cindy managed to get out between gasps of laughter. "I never saw anyone…turn that white."

Brenna drank some water, trying to calm herself, then almost choked as she laughed again. "Think how surprised she was when her wonderful new boyfriend jumped out of bed and ran out the front door, never to be seen again."

"At least we have that," Cindy said. "At least we have the satisfaction of having humiliated Marvin."

"I will savor the memory always," Sonya said with mock reverence, sending the other two into more peals of laughter.

Adam clapped his hands together and joined in the laughter, though he could not possibly have a clue what was so funny. Luke couldn't help himself. He laughed, too.

"It's good to keep a sense of humor about it all," he commented. It was nice to see a smile on Cindy's face and some color in her cheeks.

"So, what's our next move?" Cindy asked.

"Our next move is to let the appropriate law-enforcement officials handle things," Luke said sternly. "Now that we've all seen what can happen when untrained citizens try to take matters into their own hands."

"Oh, you sound like some dopey educational film," Brenna groused. She produced a map from her huge purse. "Let's try and figure out where he might have gone."

Luke tried to dissuade them from continuing to chase Marvin, but they didn't listen to one word. Sonya and Brenna claimed neither of them was going home until they'd put Marvin out of commission and recovered their money.

"I have nothing else to do with my life right now," Sonya explained. "For the past few months, I did nothing but plan my wedding. If I go back home, I'll just have to *un*plan it, plus I'll have to listen to my mother tell me how stupid I am, when she was just as much fooled by Marvin as I was."

"How can you make a full-time job out of planning a wedding?" Brenna asked. "Couldn't you just hire someone to do it all for you?"

"Oh, no. Mother had to be in control of every single aspect, from the source of the shrimp used in the bisque to the exact hue of the orchids. I was reduced to the role of secretary, making all her phone calls, taking notes at appointments, getting answers to her questions."

"Why did you do that?" Cindy asked in her forthright way.

"I have no idea. I guess I liked the idea of

being the princess, the center of attention. To tell you the truth, tracking down Marvin is the most fun thing I've ever done. The least boring, anyway."

That said something about Sonya's life, Luke thought. You would think someone with Sonya's background and advantages would have nothing to complain about, that the world would be her oyster.

Brenna pushed their discarded lunch dishes aside and spread out the Louisiana map. "Okay. Does anyone know if he has any other contacts in Louisiana?"

"The phone calls to Smoky Bayou were my only clue," Cindy said.

"The only people he ever talked about with me were back in his supposed hometown of Seattle," Sonya added. "I think they were all fictitious."

"Well, the only thing I remember," Brenna said, "is that he often mentioned a New Orleans gallery owner who was going to show my jewelry. He talked as if he'd been to New Orleans. So I'm betting he might head there."

"He's got a hot car now," Cindy pointed out. "If I were him, I'd ditch the car."

"We've determined that he has several sets of plates for the Porsche," Luke added, reluctant to encourage the ladies' vigilantism but knowing he couldn't stop it. They were like a runaway train.

"So he might opt to get the car painted rather than trade it in," said Cindy. "We could target body shops within fifty or a hundred miles of here."

"That's a terrific idea!" Sonya produced a PDA that apparently had Internet capability, because soon she'd called up an online Yellow Pages and had a list of body shops right there.

"If we divide up the list," Brenna said, looking hopefully at first Cindy then Luke, "it'll go a lot faster."

"I've got until Monday morning before I have to be at work," Cindy said. "We can check out a few."

While Sonya wrote them out a list, prioritizing them according to geography, Luke ordered a slice of chocolate cream pie.

He frowned when he took his first bite. "Blech, this tastes like cardboard."

"You're just spoiled by the Miracle Café pie," said Cindy. "You know, that gives me an idea. I've lost the diner, the physical building and the employees. But I still have the recipes."

"You could open up somewhere else," Luke said, hardly believing his ears.

But in the next sentence, she disappointed him. "I was thinking of selling the recipes. I really need to generate some income."

"You could write a cookbook," Sonya suggested. "That down-home Americana stuff is very popular right now."

"Yeah, Atkins Diet backlash," Brenna said with a laugh, sneaking a bite of Luke's pie. "You're right, this is dreadful. Hey, I know. You could auction the recipes on eBay."

"Or maybe I could just sell them on the Internet. Set up my own e-store. 'Get your own piece of the Miracle Café, a Texas tradition.'"

"I like that," Sonya said.

"And it's something I could do from anywhere. I wouldn't have to be tied down. I would just need a laptop with wireless Internet and a P.O. box."

Luke bit his tongue to stop himself from objecting. He'd thought that maybe, just maybe, last night had convinced Cindy they belonged together. But why would he think that? Great sex hadn't convinced her to stay with him when they'd been kids.

But hell, he'd given her more than just sex last night. He'd opened up to her, told her things he'd never told anyone. He'd trusted her, dammit. But it wasn't enough. Nothing he had to offer was enough, apparently.

"What's the matter with you?" Brenna asked him, abruptly bringing him back to the present. "You look like you got a hold of a bad jalapeño pepper."

"Nothing," was all he said. He couldn't get anything further past his throat.

By the sixth body shop, Cindy was starting to think this escapade wasn't very much fun anymore. Doggy seemed to enjoy getting in and out of the Blazer every few minutes and exploring a new bunch of weeds and the feet of brand-new people. And Adam slept through much of it, perhaps still regaining his strength after his brief bout of sickness. But Cindy was starting to find it a chore climbing in and out of the car as the temperatures soared, facing a new set of suspicious faces, asking the same questions and getting the same blank stares and shaking heads.

"I sure hope Sonya and Brenna are having better luck," Cindy said as she sucked the last of her Pepsi through her straw. They'd elected to stop at an old-fashioned drive-in restaurant for dinner. Ordinarily she would have relished the novelty. But she was tired. And Luke... well, Luke was as quiet as she'd ever seen him.

She'd been sure that getting him out of Cottonwood and taking him on the road would open his eyes to adventure. But he seemed to be closing in on himself. Maybe she'd only convinced him that he really did hate to travel.

"Where do you want to stop for the night?" she asked, trying another conversational gambit.

"You're the travel expert. You decide."

"Are you mad at me about something? If it's about me blowing it with Marvin, I've already said I'm sorry a half dozen—"

"No, it's not that."

"Then what?"

"I'm just tired, okay? Tired and frustrated. Do you think this junk food is good for Adam?"

"He's not really eating it. He's just gumming a French fry. It's keeping him occupied until I finish eating. Then I'll feed him something more healthy."

"Okay."

They finished up their burgers in silence. Then Cindy climbed into the back seat and coaxed Adam to eat some baby meat and vegetables and a little fruit for dessert. She cleaned him up and changed his diaper while Luke read a paperback he'd brought with him. Normally he took an active interest when she did anything with Adam. He really was out of sorts.

If she didn't know better, she'd think he was sulking.

"Bennington has a couple of decent motels," she said, since he wasn't offering any suggestions. "Let's head there."

"Okay."

It was still daylight by the time they reached Bennington, Louisiana, on the Sabine River, which ran between Texas and Louisiana. They would still have a long drive tomorrow, but not ridiculous.

"The Blue Bird is a little more expensive than the River Inn," she said. "But they have nice big bathtubs."

"You should write a guidebook to cheap motels," Luke said. "It seems like you've stayed in every one."

He wasn't joking, she realized. Despite his denial, he *was* mad at her for some reason. And she didn't think it was for her foolhardy behavior this morning.

"Eight years on the road, that's a lot of motels," she agreed. "You learn to appreciate the little things. Like a bathtub that will fit two people."

He immediately turned into the parking lot

of the River Inn, and she realized she'd made a tactical error. When she'd mentioned the bathtub, she hadn't been thinking of Jim at all. Lord, Jim would never have done something so risqué as have sex in a bath. He was very much into straightforward, man-on-top sex in a bed with the lights out.

"I was thinking of you and me," she said hastily. "That's why I mentioned the bathtub. You and me," she repeated. "And I deserve to know why you're mad at me. I don't even know what I've done."

"You haven't done anything," he said. "I just want you to be something you're not. And I finally realized, sitting in that restaurant listening to you talk about running a business from the road, that you're not going to change. And much as I'd like to, I'm not going to change, either. And all the hot sex in the world isn't going to make a difference."

Okay, she got it. "I'm not really going to start an Internet business. That was just talk, pie in the sky, if you'll forgive the pun."

"Yeah, but whatever you do, you'll do it from the road. Or you'll do it so that you *can* go on the road. You're a hometown girl with wings on her feet, and I'm a former wanderer who finally found a home. And I'm not budging. How's that going to work? It can't."

A lump formed in her throat as she let it sink in that he really wanted to work something out. That he wasn't just reliving his teenage crush or trying to reclaim his youth.

"Brenna said something to me this morning that made sense."

"About us?" he asked warily.

"Yeah."

"And you're going to trust Brenna to give relationship advice?"

"All she said was we don't have to do everything by the rules. That if we really wanted, we could find some middle ground, some innovative way to work things out."

"A compromise."

"You don't have to say it like it's a dirty word."

"There are some things I won't compromise on. I don't want a part-time wife."

Wife? Where had that come from?

"Whoa. Luke, we aren't even dating."

"If we were dating, wouldn't we be doing it with the idea of a future commitment? Because if we're not, if we're just entertaining ourselves until something better comes along, I'm not interested."

That was Luke. Plan everything out to the nth degree. Don't leave any room for uncertainty or spontaneity. "Couldn't we just see where it goes? Try it out? I'm not going anywhere for a while, at least."

"So while you're stuck in Cottonwood, you'll have me as a nice diversion."

"You're just being bullheaded. I'm not saying that at all. I'm saying that I want to be with you."

"And I'm saying that three months or six months or even a year from now, when you've got the means, you'll take off."

"And *I'm* saying that by then we'll know if we want to stay together as a couple. And we'll figure something out that we can both live with. It might take some work. Maybe it won't be perfect. But no one's life is perfect."

"So why didn't we work at it before?" Luke asked softly. "I'd have done anything to keep you."

"No, you wouldn't have. Because you thought life *could* be perfect. And so did I. Now I know better. You have to work at your life to improve it. Constantly. You never get to that point where everything's working and you can just coast."

He put the Blazer back in Drive and turned around.

"Where are you going?"

"To the Blue Bird. I think this conversation would go down a lot better in a bathtub."

Chapter Fourteen

Cindy practically vibrated with anticipation as they checked into the Blue Bird, and not just because she knew they would make love again. She felt as if she'd reached some sort of milestone with Luke, that she'd finally gotten through to him. And maybe by talking it through, she'd learned something herself.

She still didn't know how or if they could ever carve out a life as a couple that would stand the test of time. She wasn't even sure they would want to. They weren't the same people they'd been ten years ago. They had more history, more life experience to incorporate into the mix. They had more now than hormones and laughter.

But, man, did she want to try. The prospect thrilled her in a way nothing else had—not even traveling. Maybe exploring a relationship could be as exciting as riding to the top of the Statue of Liberty. It could be an adventure in its own right.

Perversely, Adam picked that night to want to stay up late. He'd napped too much that day, Cindy knew, and she'd let him. She hadn't felt up to entertaining him, introducing him to new sights and sounds and smells on a constant basis. It was more exhausting traveling with a child than she'd thought it would be.

Luke, all restless energy, declared he needed to take a walk. She would have gone with him but she was trying to get Adam settled down. "I'll be back in fifteen minutes," he said with a wink.

By the time he'd returned, Adam was finally asleep. Cindy had brushed her teeth, brushed her hair until it glowed with the natural blond highlights she'd been blessed with and wrapped herself in a towel. She'd put her lavender bubble bath by the side of the tub.

He grinned when he saw her, then contributed his own ideas to their romantic evening. He had a white plastic grocery sack with him.

He pulled out a bottle of cheap red wine and a handful of purple votive candles.

"I think these are lavender," he said uncertainly. "They smell like your hair."

She took a sniff. "Yup. We'll be drowning in lavender."

They lit the candles with the motel's complimentary matches. Cindy ran warm water and created mounds of fragrant bubbles while Luke peeled off his clothes. He turned off the overhead light, reducing the room to flickering candlelight—and the intermittent flashing of the neon sign next door coming through the frosted-glass window.

For a few moments, they just stood admiring each other's bodies. He was already aroused. He closed the distance between them, slid his arms around her waist and pressed himself against her belly.

"You make me crazy."

"Then we're even." He started to kiss her but she evaded his lips. Tempting as it was to make wild, passionate love standing up, wedged between the sink and the wall, she'd set her heart on that bathtub. "The water will get cold."

He looked at the mountains of bubbles, his lips twitching with amusement. "I haven't taken a bubble bath since I was eight years old."

"Then it's high time."

The bathtub wasn't quite as big as she'd imagined. They tried several different positions, finally settling on cozying together spoon fashion at one end. She was sitting on his lap, though the deep water buoyed her so that she was almost weightless.

She wiggled to get comfortable.

"You better watch out. One false move on your part and it could all be over."

"I think you have more control than that. Mmm, that's nice."

He was nibbling her neck, running one hand through her thick hair, holding the ends out of the water.

"Let it get wet," she said.

"You want to wash it?" he asked, as if he couldn't quite believe she would waste this bath getting clean.

"I want you to wash it," she corrected him.

It was the sexiest shampoo she'd ever experienced. Luke claimed he'd never bathed with a woman, but he certainly had a knack for it. Truthfully, Cindy was just following her instincts, as she'd never shared a tub with anyone, either.

They sudsed each other up from head to toe, incorporating massage and kisses and licks into the process. They drank wine out of plastic cups. It was like nothing Cindy had ever done before—an adventure, yet not the sort that required travel. The huge claw-foot tub in her new garage apartment would have worked.

There were adventures to be had in her own backyard, figuratively speaking, if she would simply open her eyes to them.

By the time the water started to cool, Cindy didn't think there was an inch of her skin that hadn't been thoroughly scrubbed. Luke's skin had gotten its share of attention, too.

"Shall I open the drain?" she asked, moving to her hands and knees and reaching for the lever.

"Oh, I don't think so." Luke knelt behind her, put his hands on her waist and brushed his hardness against her. "This was your idea, if I recall."

She giggled at his audacity. "I was thinking of this more as a prelude."

"Think again. I've got you all warm and naked and soapy-slick, and you think I'm not going to take advantage?" He pressed closer, his rock-hard arousal poised to enter her. But he waited for her to give him a sign that she was ready, that she was okay with this unconventional approach.

That little bit of common courtesy did her in. How many men would even consider the woman's sensibilities when he had her in this position?

She pushed back, sighing deeply as he entered her. Oh, she was so, so ready for this. Luke leaned across her back, pulling her even closer with one hand and supporting them both with the other. What should have been a bizarre posture became perfectly natural, comfortable even, their bodies almost floating in the lukewarm water as her mind floated on a cloud of pure ecstasy.

"Are you okay?" Luke asked.

"More than okay." Everything she'd ever known about making love took a new twist. Each sensation seemed new, the delicate friction between their gently rocking bodies raising her to new heights of passion. She felt truly one with Luke, as if they shared one mind orchestrating their movements, their breathing in sync, rising to a lilting crescendo like violin and cello in a symphony.

Her cries echoed against the tile, mingling with Luke's. And when it was over and they fell back into the water like a couple of satisfied sea otters, she was so limp she was afraid she might drown.

Luke maneuvered her around until they were face-to-face again and kissed her gently. They didn't have to speak. In fact, words might have just spoiled everything.

He stood up, then helped her to her feet and wrapped her in a towel. They dried each other off, blew out the candles and left their steamy cocoon.

Cindy checked on Adam—he was sleeping soundly in another borrowed crib. Then she and Luke crawled into the bed, pulled the covers up and drifted into sleep wrapped in a warm, lavender-scented cocoon.

It was with a sense of renewed optimism that Luke and Cindy set out for home the next morning. They stopped at a roadside produce stand and bought peaches and strawberries for breakfast, which they ate parked under an ancient live oak tree dripping with Spanish moss. They opened the back of the Blazer and sat on the tailgate while Adam chased a butterfly and Doggy ran wild.

"Maybe if we're lucky she'll run away," said Luke, who'd been unhappy to discover that the pup had used one of his shoes for a chew toy during the night.

"You knew better than to leave anything out

where she could get hold of it. She's a chewing machine." Even as Cindy spoke, Doggy had found a stick to shred. "And she's not about to run away. She's figured out which side her bread is buttered on."

They lingered a while longer. Cindy fed Adam his favorite cereal with apples and took delight as he noticed a squirrel chattering in the tree and pointed excitedly, yelling "Skuh, skuh!" He was starting to interact more with his world every day. Before too long she would be having actual two-way conversations with him, she thought excitedly, swinging him up in her arms as he laughed. Then he would be into even more trouble than now. She couldn't wait.

She looked over at Luke to find him studying her and Adam, an almost needy look in his eyes. Could he accept another man's child as his own? He'd said he didn't need to pass on his genes to make his world complete, but it was easier to mouth such things than to live them sometimes. Yet she wanted to find out if he could.

The next town they drove through was called Big Water, but it was hardly more than a wide place in the road with one traffic light and a dilapidated downtown—and no sign of water, big or small. "Maybe it was once near the river, and the river changed course," Cindy theorized. "Look at that old movie theater. Bet that was once the hot spot in town."

"Who still lives here, I wonder?"

"People who were born here, I'm sure. People who—oh, my God, stop the car."

Luke slammed on the brakes. "What?"

"Back up." She peered through the passenger window, wondering if she'd hallucinated. But no, there it was. A yellow Porsche parked behind a gas station/repair shop alongside several broken-down-looking vehicles.

"I'll be damned," Luke murmured. "Is that it?" He pulled the Blazer into the gas station.

"Yup. He knew we'd be looking for it."

"Hell, the FBI is looking for it now. He was smart to get rid of it."

A man in greasy overalls eyed them suspiciously as they got out. "Help you folks?"

Luke introduced himself and flashed his badge. "The man who sold you that Porsche— he's wanted."

"Aw, man, you aren't gonna tell me the car's stolen, are you?"

"Not sure about that," Luke said. "We're interested in the man, though, not the car. When did he leave and what did he leave in?"

"Or is he still in town?" Cindy asked. "Perhaps shacked up with a blonde?"

The mechanic flashed a lascivious smile. "You his wife?"

"Never mind that," Luke said. "We need to find this man. He's a dangerous fugitive." He was exaggerating a bit, but Cindy could see his ploy had the desired effect. The mechanic's eyes leaped with excitement. Probably the most exciting thing to happen in this town in decades.

"Jumpin' Jehosephat! Let's see now, he was in here late yesterday afternoon. Said he'd sell me the car cheap if I'd pay him cash. He had all the proper papers and identification."

"What name was he using?" Luke asked.

"Uh, Marvin, I believe. Uh, yup, Marvin Carter."

"Well, that's a miracle," Cindy grumbled. "His real name."

"Probably the name on the title," Luke said. "So chances are it wasn't stolen."

"We went over to the bank just before it closed, I got him his money and he left. On foot."

Cindy looked at Luke. "Probably hitchhiked. He'll get far away from here, then pay cash for another car. Damn, there won't be any way to track him."

Luke reported what they'd found out to his Louisiana FBI-agent contact. Then Cindy called Brenna and Sonya to give them the bad news. The search was off until they had another lead.

"Why don't y'all come back to Cottonwood?" she asked impulsively. "We can regroup, do some brainstorming, maybe come up with another way to track him down."

"Maybe we will," Sonya said, sounding on the verge of tears. "Lord knows I can't go home."

"Why not?" Cindy asked.

"Oh, it's complicated. So maybe we'll see you tomorrow. What's that restaurant you're working at? Ed's Mexican Food?"

"Ed's Enchilada Emporium," Cindy corrected her. "And I wouldn't recommend eating there until I get a few things sorted out."

Cindy was actually glad to see the Cottonwood city-limits sign. When she'd been on the road with Jim, her truck *was* her home, so there wasn't much opportunity to feel homesick. Now, however, she was sort of glad to be back to the familiar. She was anxious to sleep in her own bed, to be able to prepare her own meals in her own kitchen. Even if none of it really belonged to her, but to Luke.

She wasn't turning into a homebody, she reassured herself. She'd had fun on this trip, even given the fright of Adam's illness and the disappointing results of their search for Marvin. But Cottonwood wasn't a bad town, especially compared to some of the depressing burgs they'd traveled through. She could see why people wanted to live here, at least some of the time.

It was late by the time Luke pulled the Blazer into his driveway. He helped her unload the car, then paused in the middle of the driveway.

"What's wrong?" she asked, heading for the steps leading up to her carriage-house apartment with a sleepy Adam in her arms.

"Oh. Nothing." He picked up her backpack and diaper bag and followed.

About halfway up the steps, Cindy realized with a start what had been going through Luke's mind. He'd been wondering if she wanted to take everything to her apartment or just move back in with him. Since they were sleeping together.

Oh, Luke. Now that they were back in the real world, things were more complex. Were they a couple, an item? Did she take for granted they would sleep together? Should they try to hammer out their differences before letting things get out of hand, or just take it one day at a time?

He left to do his own unpacking while she bathed and fed Adam. But he came back, their leftover wine from last night in one hand and two cut-glass wineglasses in the other.

"Oh, I better not," she said, though mightily tempted. "I have to get up early—oh, shoot, all right, one glass. I'm pretty wound up from the drive."

They sat outside on the steps, with Cindy one step below, lounging between Luke's knees. Doggy clamored up and down the steps, trying to get them to play with her. Cindy obliged the pup by throwing her rawhide. No one had taught Doggy how to fetch; she just did it naturally.

"Guess she's a retriever, after all," Cindy said. "She sure is a good dog. I can't believe someone just let her wander away and didn't try to find her."

"Maybe she chewed up one too many shoes."

Cindy laughed and sipped her wine, enjoying the quiet. She hated to upset their serenity, but she had to get this out in the open or she would lie awake worrying about it tonight.

"Luke, are we back together?"

"That would depend on you," he said, trying to sound casual. But she caught the tension in his voice. He was as worried about all this as she was. "I don't consider this weekend some temporary fling," he went on. "I wasn't trying to satisfy my curiosity or get you out of my system. I'd like to find out what we could be together now that we're all grown up."

"Even if it means we might end up hurting each other again?"

"Did I hurt you before?" he asked, sounding surprised.

"Well, yeah." How could he not know that?

"You didn't act like you were hurt."

"I didn't want you to know. But when I ran off with Jim so fast—well, it was partly because I needed to get away from Cottonwood, where I wouldn't keep seeing you all the time."

"It was your choice to break up."

She set her glass down with a clunk and swiveled around to look at him. "You honestly believe that? Who said, 'Either we get married or it's over'?"

"Who said, 'Either drop everything and become a hobo with me or it's over'?" he countered.

"I doubt I used the word *hobo*."

"You wanted to wander around the world when we had no money and no jobs."

"That's not true. I had lots of ideas for jobs. I wanted to work on a cruise ship. And I'm sure I didn't make it an ultimatum."

"Not in those words. But that's what you meant. Your first priority was to leave."

"And your first was to stay."

Luke surprised her by laughing. "I guess we were pretty pigheaded, both of us."

"Yeah." She settled back between his legs. "Are we still?"

"At least we're talking about stuff. That's an improvement." He paused, drank his wine, refilled his glass. "Okay, here's my idea. You're stuck in Cottonwood for the time being, at least until you get back on your feet financially. While you're here, we can be together. And I will try very hard to accept the idea that at some point you're going to have the means to follow your dream. And I won't try to stop you, regardless of my personal feelings about it."

Cindy's eyes filled and her throat closed up. He was trying. He was really, really trying to offer a compromise of some sort. She knew what it cost him. And his effort inspired her to try a little harder herself.

"If you really mean that," she said, "then I

will try, while I'm here, to enjoy being a hometown girl. Not just tolerate but really love it. I will try to…" Did she dare say it? "I will try to grow some roots."

Luke set his glass down and wrapped his arms around her shoulders, snuggling his head against hers. "You're an incredible woman, Cindy."

His praise warmed her even more than the wine. "You're not so bad yourself. Although you'd be even better naked."

He laughed. "Does that mean negotiations are over for the evening?"

"It means we're moving into a whole new round of negotiations. Do you like the left or the right side of the bed?"

Chapter Fifteen

Cindy's newfound determination to take root in Cottonwood lasted about fifteen minutes into her first day as "assistant manager" of Ed's Enchilada Emporium.

Despite what he'd said, Ed obviously did not want her help.

"We have to start with the food," Cindy said as she inspected the kitchen, which Manson used to keep spotless and gleaming. It was now coated in grease and burned cheese, with pots left soaking in the sink, dirty utensils scattered about. "For one thing, if a restaurant inspector sets foot in here, he's going to shut us down instantly. I can see half a dozen sanitation and food-storage violations without even trying."

"That's my son's fault," Ed said angrily. "He's supposed to keep this place clean." He stepped over to the back door, which was open to let in the morning breeze or they would have suffocated on stale, burned food odors. Cindy noticed a hole in the screen door that hadn't been there three weeks ago. Flies would be pouring in. She wrote a reminder in her notebook, which was already full of reminders: *Fix screen.*

"Hey, Arnie!" Ed screamed out the back door. "Put down that Game Boy and get in here and scrub down this kitchen. What do you think I'm paying you for?"

Ed's entire family was on the staff—his wife, his brother, his sister, his three grown children and his mother-in-law. Although Cindy had yet to look at the books, she suspected payroll alone would bankrupt the place before long. Ed didn't have enough business to warrant so many full-time employees.

But first things first. "Why don't we go over the menu?" she suggested mildly.

The menu was handwritten, decorated with colored markers and photocopied. It was a cute idea to give the restaurant that family-business, we're-just-folks appeal. Unfortunately it was poorly executed. Whoever had designed it had bad handwriting and couldn't spell. She voiced her opinions about the menu as delicately as she could.

"My daughter designed that menu," Ed exploded. Cindy was quickly realizing that he seldom spoke without exploding. Not her idea of a dream boss.

"We need to take it to a professional graphic artist to take your daughter's very creative design and execute it in a more customer-intuitive style." She didn't really know what a *customer-intuitive* style was, but she figured maybe if she threw a few big words at Ed, he might believe she knew what she was doing. "But first, we need to decide a few things about the dishes you're serving."

"There's nothing wrong with these dishes," he said stubbornly. "These are my wife's grandmother's recipes. Helena grew up in Leon, Mexico."

And Grandma had a fondness for mole sauce apparently, because the unsweetened, chocolaty goo was in everything, on every dish. "I'm sure that your grandmother was a wonderful cook. And mole sauce would go over well in, say, Dallas, where the palates are more sophisticated. But we're in east Texas. It's all right to have a few fancy, innovative dishes on the menu." Shoot, her friends and neighbors could probably stand to try something new once in a while. "But the majority of the menu should be basic Tex-Mex and not too hot."

"Mexican food's not supposed to be served bland," Ed said.

"I agree. I personally love intense flavors. But you have to play to your audience. If you load every dish with mole sauce and jalapeño peppers, you're not going to get a lot of repeat business."

And that, she realized during the first lunch shift, was the basic problem. Diners would put up with surly, incompetent waiters and a slow kitchen, even high prices, if the food was any good. And it wasn't. She tasted everything being prepared in the kitchen, and most of it was so hot it nearly took her head off. And she *liked* spicy food.

She tried to offer advice to the head cook, Mrs. LaRue—Helena—but she spoke almost no English. Her daughter, who helped out in the kitchen, tried to translate, but either Helena still didn't understand or she chose not to. She acted as if she were deaf to anyone but Ed.

Eventually Cindy gave up. She put on an

apron and filled in for the wait staff, who spent most of their time on break standing just outside the back door, smoking. Not that there was really much to do. During the lunch rush, the restaurant had exactly three tables filled. At two of them sat people she didn't know—possibly visitors here to look at lake property or shop for antiques at Cottonwood's many shops. Poor saps, no one had told them to stay away.

At the third table were Brenna, Sonya—and Luke. When had he come in? As she walked over to their booth to give him a menu, she felt an irrational streak of jealousy seeing him cozied up with those two attractive blondes. Amazing how quickly she had become proprietary. Their relationship was, what, two days old?

"I'll give you this just in case you can decipher little Lupe's chicken scrawl," she said to Luke, handing him the menu. "Otherwise, I redid the chalkboard with some specials. If you don't like jalapeños and mole, you're out of luck."

Luke looked worried. "I take it things aren't going well?"

She sighed. "It's only the first day. Maybe I have to win Ed's confidence before he'll listen to me."

"I love jalapeños and mole sauce," Brenna said. "How about those chicken enchiladas?"

"Not if you knew how the chicken's been stored. You're risking ptomaine. Go with the beef. We just got our shipment of beef this morning."

"Is the hamburger safe?" Luke asked.

"If I can convince Mama LaRue to hold the peppers."

"What about the tortilla soup?" Sonya asked.

"That's actually not half-bad." Cindy wrote down their choices, headed for the kitchen, then stopped in the middle of the dining room wondering why they were here together. She returned to their table. "Is there any news?"

"We hope so," said Sonya, venturing an almost smile.

"I just got a call from Shelly," said Luke. "You know, the bank teller from Faring?"

Cindy's heart hammered so loud inside her chest, she was sure everyone could hear it. "And…?"

"She's coming here to talk to me," Luke continued. "She said she wanted to tell me something, that I was the only one she trusted. She's scared of the FBI man and she doesn't trust Sheriff Tucker."

"And she's coming all the way here to tell you in person?"

"Apparently so. I think she was protecting Marvin before. We all thought she knew more than she was telling, that maybe Marvin had told her where he was going or where to find him if he suddenly left town."

Cindy scooted into the booth next to Brenna. "This is great! Oh, Luke, you have to catch that SOB—you just have to." She dropped her voice to a whisper. "I'm trying to like my job, I really am, but this is torture. I'm used to being in charge here. Now no one will listen to me. One of Ed's kids even cussed at me when I suggested he tuck his shirt in."

Luke's face hardened. "Where is the little jerk?"

"No, no, I don't need you to rescue me. I can handle the LaRues. Just get my money back, please, so I don't have to work here."

"I'm doing my best."

Luke was a bundle of nerves as he escorted Shelly Bernard into his office. She'd arrived in a slick silver Infiniti, nicer than a bank teller could afford. A present from her rich daddy? No wonder Marvin had targeted her.

She pulled a rolling suitcase out of the trunk, which Luke stepped forward to help with.

"Um, Ms. Bernard, if you're hoping I'll offer you sanctuary here, I can't do it. If you've aided and abetted a felon, I don't have the power to protect you from prosecution."

"I already told you I didn't know he was a criminal when I started hanging out with him," she said in a scared voice. "I thought he was a computer salesman."

Luke knew that. Furthermore, he believed her, knowing Marvin Carter's history. He just wanted to put the fear of God into her, in case she had any ideas about misdirecting him. Now he changed tack. He was the good cop, bad cop all rolled into one.

"Ms. Bernard, I know you must be scared," he said after they'd settled into his office. "And hurting. Marvin Carter is one of the most skilled con men I've ever encountered. The other women he swindled were smart, confident, self-sufficient women like you, so there's no need to feel embarrassed that he fooled you, too.

"I want to help you," he continued. "No one wants you to get in trouble. We just want to catch this guy and stop him from hurting other women."

"You don't want to arrest me?" she asked, on the verge of tears.

"Not if you cooperate." Luke leaned forward, speaking almost in a whisper. "Do you know where he is?"

Shelly shook her head. "No, I really don't. I wasn't lying about that. I wasn't lying about anything, really. I just didn't believe Des—I mean, Marvin—was a criminal. Until I found this." She hoisted the suitcase onto Luke's desk. "He'd put it under my bed. I thought it was just his clothes. But then he called me and wanted me to bring 'his things' to him."

Luke's heart beat a little faster. "He called you?" The FBI had put a wiretap on Shelly's home phone, with her reluctant permission.

"On my cell phone. And he was calling from *his* cell phone. That's hard to trace, isn't it?"

Luke nodded, disappointed. "So where did he want you to bring 'his things'?"

"Well, we never got that far. I was so dumb—I should have pretended to cooperate with him. But instead I got mad and he hung up. That was when I jimmied the lock on his suitcase. Go ahead, see what's inside."

Luke put on a pair of thin rubber gloves, so as to not add his fingerprints to the mix, and opened the suitcase. His eyes nearly popped out of his head. The case was stuffed full of cash—stacks and stacks of fifties, twenties and tens.

"I counted it," Shelly said. "It's three hundred thousand dollars, give or take. It came out a little different every time I counted. And it's all there, every penny," she added almost proudly. "I didn't even take any to buy gas to get over here."

Luke realized how hard it must have been for Shelly, how tempting it would have been to take some or all of the money. He also realized something else. This cash undoubtedly represented the proceeds from the sale of the Miracle Café. Luke had recently learned from Anne Hardison, a lawyer who was helping him follow leads, that Marvin had received a cashier's check for the full amount, then cashed it.

This was Cindy's money.

Luke thanked Shelly profusely. He assured her that she wouldn't be prosecuted, that she'd done everything right, though she hadn't.

"I should have arranged a meeting with him," she said bleakly. "Then you could have caught him."

"That would have been ideal," Luke agreed. "But you did the night thing by handing over the suitcase." He wrote out a receipt for the suitcase and the cash, though Shelly didn't seem to have any expectation she would see it again. Then he encouraged her to go back home.

He didn't want her running into any of The Blondes, as he'd started to think of them. He wanted to be the one to break the good news to Cindy that she would be getting at least a portion of her money back.

When Luke heard the front door open, he hurriedly zipped the suitcase shut and stuck it under his desk, then peeled off the gloves. He had to think about what to do next. The FBI would have to be notified. He should probably talk to Anne, too. Anne would know how to proceed in a way that would protect Cindy's right to that money.

One week after she'd started working for Ed's Enchilada Emporium, Cindy got her first look at Ed LaRue's accounting books. He'd promised several times to sit down with her and go over the finances. But he always claimed he was too busy. Now, on a day when he'd stayed home, supposedly sick, she was taking matters into her own hands. As the assistant manager, she had a right to know something about the finances, she reasoned. And it wasn't as if Ed had told her she couldn't look.

What she saw was ten times worse than she had imagined. Not only was Ed's in a negative cash-flow situation but he was siphoning money out of the business account. Not in some sneaky way but blatantly. In addition to the salaries he paid his family employees, he wrote checks willy-nilly to pay for personal expenses that had nothing to do with the restaurant.

At this rate, Ed's would be bankrupt in no time. And she would be out of a job and possibly held responsible for the restaurant's failure, since she'd been hired to fix things. But it was kind of hard to fix things when Ed refused to follow any of her advice. She was basically a glorified waitress.

No wonder Ed hadn't wanted to go over the books. She would be lucky if she got even one paycheck out of him.

She tried not to let it bother her. Other than her shaky financial situation, her life wasn't so bad right now. In fact, things were pretty good.

And Luke was the reason.

She got all warm and gooey inside when she thought of Luke. He'd been such a help to her this past week as she'd struggled to establish a routine. He was the one who picked up Adam from Polly's each afternoon, since her hours were long and erratic. When she got home from work each night, usually late, he would pamper her, rub her feet, pour her a glass of wine or a cup of herbal tea.

He took her out to the movies. They cooked together. Then he would spend the night at her place, so that Adam's routine didn't have to be disrupted. He was always thinking of Adam, so she didn't even bother to argue that Adam didn't mind having his routine interrupted.

They made love every single night. Even when she was dog tired, she had no trouble summoning the energy for sex. She'd never experienced anything like the intimacy she shared with Luke—wild and adventurous, then tender and sweet. Nothing like the safe, dependable sex she'd had with Jim or Marvin's polished but bloodless seductions.

She'd thought she knew Luke. But the man had depths she never imagined, layers and layers to be peeled away. Exploring his collection of books had been an eye-opener. He'd discovered reading in college, and his current tastes ran to some pretty heavy stuff—James Joyce, Ayn Rand, Alice Sebold. He'd gotten her excited about reading, too, and she realized she could enjoy vicarious adventures when she couldn't actually travel.

She could spend years getting to know the

man Luke had become, and her lust for adventure responded to that challenge.

On his day off, he'd painted circus animals in the corner where Adam's crib was set up. He'd gotten some kit from a craft store and done it to surprise them. Then yesterday, her first and only day off in a week, the weather had turned unexpectedly warm, their last breath of summer before winter really set in. They'd dug in the garden, all four of them—she and Luke, Adam and Doggy.

It was all so disgustingly domestic. And Cindy had, to her surprise, enjoyed it immensely. Now this little voice inside her was trying to convince her that settling down wouldn't be such a bad thing.

She fought it. She'd thought of herself as a traveler/adventuress for so many years now that it was nearly impossible to believe she could be a contented small-town dweller. And she wasn't giving up her dream of traveling, not really. She was just toying with the idea that she could scale it down some. That during the times when she couldn't travel, living in Cottonwood—with Luke—wouldn't exactly be torture.

When someone knocked on Ed's office door, Cindy quickly put away the accounting book and bank statement. The door opened and Ed's wife, Helena, barged in, scowling with suspicion.

"What are you doing in here?" she asked in surprisingly perfect English.

"Just some paperwork," Cindy asked, irritated that her motives would be questioned. She was beginning to wonder if Helena's problems with English were simply an act so she wouldn't have to listen or talk to Cindy. "Is there something I can do for you?"

"I run out of mole," she said. "I cannot buy in this stupid, backward town."

Cindy bristled at anyone calling Cottonwood stupid and backward. She could think it herself, but that was different. She'd grown up here. She didn't like it coming from an outsider. "As I explained, I can order your more exotic ingredients online, but it may take up to a week to get here."

"A week!" Helena screeched. "I need *now*. You go to Tyler or Dallas and buy for me *now*."

Cindy's first instinct was to object to being ordered about like one of the LaRue children. But then she realized what a golden opportunity this was. The boss's wife was *ordering* her to leave town right in the middle of a workday. She could do with a nice long drive and some shopping.

"I'll go right now," she said with a smile, which apparently irritated Helena that much more. "Please write down exactly what you need." Although privately Cindy thought that running out of mole would be the best thing that could happen to Ed's Enchilada Emporium.

A few minutes later, with a list from Mama LaRue, the restaurant checkbook and a heady sense of freedom, Cindy headed out into the pleasantly cool afternoon. On a whim, she decided to swing by Polly's and pick up Adam. He could probably use an outing, too.

When she pulled up in front of Polly's house, she saw that the older toddlers, Michelle and Ben, were on the swing set in the front yard, taking advantage of the gorgeous weather and shrieking at the tops of their lungs.

Cindy loved that sound, she realized. The older Adam got, the more noise he made— and he was getting to the point that he actually laughed and talked a little, sounding more like a child than a baby. She loved his laughter. Luke seemed to take great delight in making Adam laugh.

Polly sat on the wide front porch with Adam

in her lap. She managed to hold him and shell peas at the same time.

"Hello, there!" Polly called out with a jaunty wave.

Cindy waved back, then unhooked the latch on the chain-link gate to let herself in the yard. As she did, a rambunctious ball of black fur hurled itself across the yard and jumped up against her legs, begging for attention.

"Doggy, what are you doing here?" she asked, encouraging the pup to get down before she would pet her. The dog followed on her heels as she made her way to the porch and up the steps. "Hi, Polly. Hi, Adam!" Adam reached his arms to her and she picked him up. "Did Luke sucker you into taking care of Doggy, too?" The pup did tend to chew things up if left alone for long periods.

"What?" Polly looked at her, puzzled.

"I was just wondering what Luke's dog was doing here."

"Oh, um, that's not Luke's. He's mine. Barky. I made the mistake of letting the kids name him."

Cindy set Adam down and took a closer look at the puppy. Sure enough, it was a boy. But in every other respect he was identical to Doggy, right down to the white star on his chest.

"Do you want some lemonade?" Polly asked, putting the peas aside and hoisting herself out of her rocker.

Cindy recognized a ploy to distract her when she saw one. "You got this dog from Mike, didn't you? One of his labs jumped a fence and had a litter of mongrel pups."

"Um, well, yes, that's where we got Barky."

"And Doggy. Luke planted that puppy under a bush at his house knowing Adam wouldn't be able to resist. Knowing *I* would fall in love with it."

Polly wrung her hands like a silent-movie melodrama queen. "Oh, now, Cindy, he didn't mean anything by it. He just thought Adam needed a dog and he knew you wouldn't consent. And after all, the pup does belong to Luke. It's not like he forced it on you."

"It's not the dog I object to," Cindy said, grappling with her feeling of disappointment, probably all out of proportion to the situation. "It's the underhandedness of it all. Why did he have to lie to me about it?" But she knew the answer. If he'd brought home a puppy out of the blue, she would have seen through him immediately.

As it was, it had simply taken her a bit longer to realize what a sneak he was. His plan was to get Adam attached to the puppy—so attached that Cindy would have a hard time dragging Adam away. He'd wanted to trap her in Cottonwood.

"Oh, Cindy, just look at your face. Come on, now, it was just a harmless ruse."

Cindy shook her head. "No, it wasn't. He says he's willing to compromise. He says he wouldn't try to keep me here if I need to go. But all the while, he was coming up with every way he could think of to tie me down to Cottonwood. Fixing up the apartment, getting me the job, the garden, the circus animals—"

"Circus animals?" Polly asked, apparently picturing zebras and elephants penned in Luke's backyard.

"On the wall," Cindy answered distractedly. She sank onto the top porch step, absently petting Barky. Adam threw his arms around her neck, sensing she needed comfort.

"Oh, honey." Polly sat next to Cindy, sliding an arm around her shoulders. "Maybe he was being sneaky. But it's because he loves you. He's got you back and he can't bear the thought of losing you again."

"If he really loved me, he wouldn't try to make me into something I'm not. He wouldn't try to stifle an important part of me."

"I don't think he sees it that way."

"No. The way he sees it is that he knows what's best for me and for Adam. He's never understood that restless part of me. So he's determined to stamp out what he doesn't understand. It's typical, provincial, small-town tunnel vision."

Polly didn't have an answer for that, so she came back with the only argument she could come up with. "Luke is a good man, Cindy. Not perfect, maybe, but good. You let him get away once. If I were you, I'd think long and hard before I tossed him away again."

Chapter Sixteen

Cindy found the things Helena needed at a specialty food shop in Tyler. She paid twice what she would have paid her Internet supplier, but she took no joy in being right. In fact, she took no joy in anything—not the fine weather, not Adam's excited verbalization of "Bird, bird!" when he saw a caged parrot in a pet store, not even the fact that she was free for a few hours from Ed's.

It felt as if her whole life had a big storm cloud over it, and she couldn't escape it with any amount of driving.

On the way back to Cottonwood, she saw something that intrigued her. It was a small camper parked in the front yard of a house not much bigger than her apartment. And it had a faded For Sale sign tacked to it.

It couldn't hurt to ask. She had no money in the bank, but maybe the owners were anxious to sell and would let her write a promissory note or something. She pulled into the gravel drive and cut the engine.

The woman who answered the door had a malnourished look about her. Her age was hard to determine—somewhere between thirty and forty. She introduced herself as Nancy and eagerly showed Cindy the camper.

"Davey and I went all over the place in this thing," she said wistfully. "Flea markets, trade shows. Davey was a whittler. Carved little animals. Made just enough money to keep us going."

"It sounds like a wonderful life," Cindy said, meaning it.

"It was for a while. But a woman gets a hankering to settle down, you know? Put down some roots? Have a few kids?" She smiled at Adam, tousled his hair.

"And is that what you did?"

She shook her head. "Davey couldn't sit still for long. When it came to choosing between me and his freedom, well…" Nancy shrugged. "I don't blame him none."

Cindy boiled over with righteous indignation. Of course she should blame him. Nancy's desire to have a permanent home and raise a family was perfectly understandable, and Davey should have—

She stopped herself before she started to feel very, very foolish. She should be identifying with Davey, not Nancy. He was a free spirit, just like her. But for some reason she was seeing everything through Nancy's point of view.

The camper was tiny but very cute and well maintained. Just enough room for two or three people. If only she had some skill that would translate into quick cash at trade shows and flea markets. Maybe she could set up a Miracle biscuit booth. Miracle biscuits could become the next funnel cakes. Or pies might be even better.

Yeah, right. She had nowhere near the funds needed to buy the camper, and since she could plainly see that Nancy needed the cash, she didn't even try to talk the other women into a deferred-payment deal. She thanked Nancy, and she and Adam were on their way back home.

Home. Yes, that was how she'd started to think of Cottonwood. In all the years of growing up there and in the time since she and Jim had bought the house, the word *home* had just never sat well with her. Now, strangely enough, when she was more trapped than ever, she actually looked forward to cozying up in her little apartment.

Of course, she would have to face off with Luke about his deception. She couldn't let that one fester. But even that proposition wasn't as horrible as it had seemed earlier. She had a good thing going with Luke. There were millions of women like Nancy who would give their right arm to have a guy like Luke, a settling-down, constant, reliable guy. She would never have to worry about Luke getting restless and taking off for parts unknown.

"Maybe I overreacted about the puppy, huh, Adam?" she said, for lack of an adult to talk to. But Adam was asleep.

It was almost five by the time Cindy reached Cottonwood. She stopped by Ed's to deliver her purchases to Helena and to make sure there were no disasters. But how disastrous could things get when there were no customers? She put Arnie, Ed's oldest son, in charge, then left for the evening. She'd been told when Ed hired her that she wouldn't have to work most evenings. So tonight, when he wasn't there to object, she was taking off. She stopped at the grocery store to buy some pork chops and a few other ingredients she would need to fix a nice dinner for Luke. Then they would hash out this business about his sneakiness. And maybe they would hash out some other things, too.

For the first time ever, she let herself admit she wanted a future with Luke. She didn't want to end up like poor Nancy—or poor Davey, wherever he was. He was probably as miserable as she was. So Cindy was going to put all her cards on the table, and they were going to work out some arrangement they both could live with.

Grubb's Food Mart was crowded, and Cindy had to wait in line at the checkout. She reached for a magazine just as another woman did the same. Their hands bumped and they laughed. Then Cindy realized the other woman was Anne Hardison, the attorney who'd been trying to help them track down Marvin. She was a redheaded beauty who'd married one of the very eligible Hardison boys a couple of years before. She had a darling little girl, Olivia, just a couple of months older than Adam. The two babies were already eyeing each other with interest from their respective shopping carts.

"Cindy, I didn't realize it was you."

Cindy smiled. Anne had been something of an outsider in high school, and Cindy had been one of the ones to snub her. But they'd become friends recently, and Cindy couldn't imagine what she'd found not to like when they were younger. "It's good to see you, Anne. I've been meaning to call and thank you for all the work you've done."

"I don't know why. You and The Blondes had more success than me or any of the law-enforcement people trying to find Marvin."

"The Blondes?"

Anne blushed. "Sorry. That's what Luke calls them. Oh, look, isn't that cute?"

Their two children were babbling at each other, sounding for all the world like a real conversation, and maybe it was.

"We should get these two together for a play-date," Cindy said, still pondering The Blondes.

"I bet you're happy to be getting your money back. No more working for Ed LaRue."

Cindy gave Anne a blank look. "Excuse me?"

"The crime lab is about done with the cash. They wanted to keep it longer, but I pointed out the very clear paper trail indicating that money came directly from the sale of the restaurant," Anne chattered on, oblivious to the fact that Cindy's mouth was hanging open in astonishment.

The customer ahead of her finished her

transaction, and the man behind her with only two cantaloupes and a bottle of soda cleared his throat.

"You go ahead of me," Cindy said distractedly, moving her basket aside. "Anne, what money?"

Anne's eyes widened. "The cash…in the suitcase?"

"I have no idea what you're talking about."

Now Anne looked sheepish. "I guess Luke hasn't told you about it yet."

"What cash in what suitcase?" Cindy demanded, her face growing warm.

Now the customer ahead of Anne moved on, and Anne had to pull her basket out of line, too. She looked a little scared. "I think you should get the story from Luke."

Cindy put her hand on Anne's arm. She hadn't meant to take her anger out on Anne, who she was sure was a completely innocent party. "Anne, I need you to tell me."

"Um, Shelly, the bank teller, showed up last Monday with a suitcase full of cash. Three hundred thousand dollars. I'm sure Luke didn't tell you because he wanted to be sure—"

Cindy didn't wait to hear the rest. She pulled a bewildered Adam from the shopping cart, grabbed her purse, abandoned her groceries and headed for her car.

* * *

Luke had taken off early from work that afternoon and had stopped at the grocery store for some pork chops. Cindy was a much better cook than him, and she could throw together a mouthwatering home-cooked meal in thirty minutes, where it would take him two hours. But it wasn't fair to always expect her to cook when she worked more hours than he did and had a child to care for on top of everything else. Tonight he intended to treat her.

He wasn't at all sure a home-cooked meal would get him back into her good graces. Polly had called to warn him that Cindy was on the warpath. She'd found out where Doggy had come from and she was really mad he'd tried to pull one over on her.

He probably should have told her the truth about the pup. But she would have seen exactly what he'd been trying to do, purposely getting Adam attached to a dog so it would be harder to drag him away. Still, if he'd fessed up early on, he wouldn't be facing this uncomfortable confrontation now.

He was hoping, though, that once Cindy heard the good news, she would forget all about being mad at him.

She burst through his kitchen door just as he put the pork chops in the oven.

"Hi, gorgeous. How was your—" He stopped short when he saw the thundercloud that was Cindy's face. She was madder about this puppy thing than he'd figured.

"Can I get you a nice glass of wine?" he asked pleasantly, as if she weren't glaring shards of broken glass at him.

Without a word she took Adam into the living room, where Luke had set up a safe play area. She apparently didn't want him to witness the battle that was about to take place.

He had a feeling things were about to get ugly.

As soon as she returned to the kitchen, he launched into his defense, knowing that if he let her get started on a tirade he wouldn't get a word in edgewise.

"You'd never have let me give Adam a puppy," he began. "But you have to agree, the boy needed a dog. I had to be a little underhanded about it. And besides, I never suggested that *you* should take responsibility for Doggy."

"You were hoping I would, though." Her words were razor sharp. "Give me something to cut up. I need to keep my hands busy."

Or she'd strangle him. She didn't need to say

the words; Luke understood perfectly well. He grabbed a cabbage, a cutting board, a knife and a bowl and set them on the kitchen table in front of her. "Coleslaw." He wasn't sure it was wise to give her a knife when she was in this mood, but he didn't think she would use it on him.

She whacked the cabbage in half with one swipe of the big blade, probably imagining it to be Luke's head. He winced and went back to mashing the potatoes he'd boiled, adding milk and plenty of butter. Damn the cholesterol. They needed comfort food.

"I'm sorry I deceived you," he said. "In retrospect, it was the wrong thing to do."

"Only because you got caught."

"I knew you'd find out eventually. I knew you'd see Barky and put two and two together. I just didn't think you'd be quite this mad about it."

"You think all this is about the puppy?"

"Well, isn't it?"

"Tell me, Luke, isn't there something else you want to get off your chest? Some other little thing that you forgot to tell me? Just by accident?"

Uh-oh. "Did you by any chance talk to Anne Hardison today?" Anne was the only other person in town who knew about the suitcase full of money—he hadn't even told The Blondes. With Cindy so busy with her new job and Anne declaring she would never set foot in Ed's Enchilada Emporium again, he hadn't thought the two women would have reason to talk.

"Why would you bring up Anne's name?" Cindy's voice dripped with sarcasm.

"I was going to tell you about the money tonight," Luke said quickly. "That's what this dinner was all about. I thought we'd celebrate."

"You've had that money for *a week.* And you're only now telling me about it? What's to stop me from believing you *never* intended to tell me?"

"Cindy, of course I was going to tell you. It's just that I didn't know until today whether you would actually get the money back. I had to turn it over to the FBI and they had to process it as evidence. Then a magistrate had to look at the paper trail and determine who the money should go to. I learned just today that the entire amount—about three hundred thousand dollars—is going to you."

At least, that was the justification he gave himself ten times a day.

Cindy said nothing, just kept hacking away at the cabbage, cutting it into smaller and smaller pieces. Pretty soon it was going to be cabbage mush, unfit for anyone but Adam.

She wasn't buying his rationale.

"All right, maybe I should have told you."

"Well, duh."

"But things were going so well. I've never been as happy as I have been this past week, being with you."

"Because you had everything your way. I was trapped here in Cottonwood, working at the job that *you* got for me, living in the apartment that *you* provided, playing with the puppy you foisted on us through deception."

"Because I knew the second you got your money back, you'd leave," he said dully. He gave up on the mashed potatoes. No one was going to eat them anyway. "I knew I'd lose you, Cindy. Was it so wrong to want to have a few more days with you?"

"I wouldn't have just left. Don't you think I put any value on what we had, what we were building?"

"If you did, you didn't give me any indication."

"I told you I was willing to compromise. But that wasn't good enough for you. You wanted me totally on your terms."

Luke didn't have a good rebuttal. Maybe she

was telling the truth. Maybe he was the in-flexible one.

"I was really mad at you about the trick you played on me with Doggy. But Polly talked to me. She said I'd thrown you away once and I shouldn't be so hasty to do so again. And I drove to Tyler and I thought and thought and I realized that you'd only done what you did because you wanted what was best for Adam. Or what you thought was best."

She laid down her knife, some of her fury dissipated. "And you know what? I was even starting to think that maybe you *did* know best. This past week was good, really good. Even working a horrible job, I was still happier than I've been in a long time. And I was starting to think settling down wasn't such an awful thing. I was ready to have it out with you about the dog, but I also was determined that we should hammer out our differences and come to a workable solution. And I was sure we could do that. Because I've changed. I don't have to have everything my way anymore.

"But Luke, you haven't changed at all. You may say you want to compromise, but your actions say something else."

She plucked a paper napkin from the holder

on the table and blotted her eyes. Then she stood up.

"Cindy, wait."

But she was already heading for the living room to collect Adam.

"Don't leave all mad. Let's talk about this."

She picked up Adam from his play area, startling him so much that he started crying. "The only reason you're willing to talk is because I've backed you into a corner. But once you got me calmed down, we'd be back where we started. I love you, Luke. I really do. But I can't forge any sort of permanent relationship with a man who's willing to lie and manipulate to get what he wants, even if he believes he's justified."

"We'll talk tomorrow, when—"

"No, we won't. I'm going to stay with Sonya and Brenna at the Kountry Kozy. You can deliver my money there. I *can* trust you to deliver it, right?"

The fact that she had to ask galled him. "Yes, of course."

She walked out without another word.

Luke plunked down at the table feeling as if a tornado had just whipped through his life, taking everything that mattered. And he had no one to blame but himself. He'd brought all this on because he'd been so sure he knew what was right for Cindy and Adam. But he'd blown it, big-time.

Doggy appeared in the kitchen doorway, having been up to no good probably. For the first time ever, she hesitated instead of galumphing toward him certain of being received enthusiastically.

He patted his leg. "Come on, girl."

She trotted to him, and he pulled her into his lap. In a few weeks, he wouldn't be able to do this anymore. The pup was growing fast. He patted her and scratched her behind her ears, the place she really liked. Poor thing, she had no idea she was at the center of any controversy. Or that her favorite playmate had been taken away for good.

Chapter Seventeen

Brenna opened the door of her room at the Kountry Kozy B and B, and for a moment, she just stared at Cindy standing in the hallway with Adam on one hip and loaded down with suitcases.

"I don't have anywhere else to go," Cindy said.

Brenna smiled knowingly and opened the door wider. "This looks like man trouble to me." She wore a pair of strange-looking jeans with holes ripped up and down the legs and a skimpy T-shirt that showed her trim waist. Her white-frosted hair was spiked so severely, it looked as if it could do injury to anyone who got too close. The nails on one foot were painted a shocking shade of purple while the others were bare.

"I won't stay under his roof one minute longer," Cindy declared as she dragged her suitcases into the large room. "If you girls won't have me, I'll have to check in at the homeless shelter in Tyler."

"Of course we'll have you," Brenna said kindly. "Us blondes have to stick together."

"Oh, so you heard Luke's clever nickname for us."

Brenna waved away Cindy's irritation. "Everyone's calling us that."

"Where's Sonya?" Cindy asked as she set Adam down on a rag rug and set out a selection of his favorite toys.

"She went for a walk. She just received some unpleasant news. Her mother has closed her Visa account."

"Uh-oh."

"Yeah, no more free ride on Mama Patterson. Frankly, I'm not sure how we're going to pay for any more nights at the B and B. Mrs. Bressler said we could stay one more, since we'd been good customers, but that's the limit of her charity."

"You don't seem too upset."

"I figure something will come up. It always does."

"Well, you're right. I can pay for the room."

"You mean you actually got a paycheck from that Ed LaRue character?"

"No, even better. Remember when Shelly came here to see Luke?"

"Yeah, then Luke wouldn't tell us what she wanted. Said it was confidential."

"She showed up with a suitcase full of cash." Cindy explained how it had all happened and how the FBI was going to give the money to her.

Cindy had been a little worried about how the other women would take her news. After all, Marvin had swindled all of them. They could justifiably lay claim to some of the cash.

But Brenna seemed happy as could be about Cindy's change of fortune. "I am so jazzed. I mean, if push comes to shove, Sonya and I both have families we can fall back on. But you don't. And you have a child to support."

"Still, I think it's only right that I share. If y'all are game, I'd like to finance our continued search for Marvin."

"Oh, girlfriend, you don't want to do that," Brenna said. She sat down on one of the double beds and resumed polishing her toenails.

"You've got the money to start a new life now, do anything you want. You could travel or buy a house or start a new business. Don't get caught up in this revenge thing against Marvin. He's not worth it."

"But you're not giving up, are you?"

Brenna hesitated. "Maybe it's time to cut our losses. I've got a jewelry show coming up next month. If I don't have some pieces ready to go by then…"

"But we came so close. Next time we'll be smarter. We won't scare him off."

"The FBI is more involved now," Brenna argued. "They're better equipped to catch a con man."

"But not nearly as motivated. I got a portion of my money back, but there's still more than a half million out there somewhere. That's my son's future."

Brenna's eyes shined with hope. "You really want to go after him? It's not just because you're mad at Luke?"

"He lied to me. Twice that I know of. He knew about the money a week ago and didn't tell me because he wanted to keep me trapped here. After Marvin, I'm not ready to deal with someone who isn't totally honest."

Brenna frowned. "I don't really know the

deputy that well, but that doesn't sound like him. He must really love you to work so hard to keep you around."

Cindy harrumphed. "I don't call it love, I call it manipulation."

"Doggy?" Adam chimed in. "Doggy?"

Cindy picked him up. "Oh, baby, Doggy's not here." She didn't have the heart to tell him that he would most likely not see Doggy ever again.

"Here's my idea," Cindy said. "I've got my eye on a travel trailer. It would be cozy, but the three of us—well, four, counting Adam—could live in it as we follow Marvin's trail."

Brenna laughed. "Uh, maybe you didn't notice, but Sonya's not exactly the travel-trailer type. See all this stuff?" Brenna pointed out suitcase after suitcase, a dresser lined with cosmetics, a wardrobe completely stuffed with clothes. "This is all Sonya's. She doesn't travel light."

Cindy sagged with disappointment. "Damn. It seemed like such a good idea at the time."

"Well, shoot, we'll ask her. Since you're going to finance this gig, if we continue, I guess you're calling the shots."

"No, I don't want it to be like that." She jiggled Adam on one knee, trying to distract him from thoughts of his puppy. "We'll make decisions together."

The click-click of a pair of high heels echoed down the hallway, coming closer. The door opened and Sonya stepped in. She looked polished as ever in crisp, tailored black pants and a mint-green cashmere sweater. Her sleek blond hair was pulled back into a fancy clip of some kind.

But her makeup was smeared. She'd been crying. She looked so desolate, in fact, that Cindy wanted to forget her troubles and put her arms around Sonya. But Sonya wasn't a real touchy-feely person, so Cindy restrained herself.

"What's going on here?" Sonya asked.

"Cindy's moving in with us," Brenna announced. "She had a fight with the deputy and she wants to go on the road with us. And, Sonya, she can pay for the whole thing."

Sonya's blue eyes filled with surprise and just a hint of hope. So Cindy repeated her story. "I'm quitting my job first thing tomorrow morning," she said. "I doubt Ed was going to be able to pay me anyway. Then as soon as I get that big check, I'm going to buy me a camper. You can stay with me or in a motel, whichever you prefer," she said for Sonya's benefit. Sonya had indeed wrinkled her nose at the mention of *camper*.

"But where will we go?" Sonya asked. "We don't have a clue where Marvin has gone."

"Shelly is the key. He's not going to give up on that suitcase full of cash so easily. I'll bet you anything he'll contact her again."

"But won't she just tell the sheriff or that FBI guy?" Brenna asked. "Why would she even talk to us?"

"She may not be ready to admit it yet, but she's one of The Blondes, too. She shares a bond with us. She's afraid of the sheriff and the FBI. She doesn't believe they're on her side. But she knows we are."

Sonya and Brenna both looked thoughtful.

"Luke?" Adam said, clear as day.

"Not now, sweetie."

The other women gave Cindy pitying looks.

"Are you sure you want to run off and leave the deputy behind?" Brenna asked.

Cindy sighed hopelessly. "Even if I could forgive him for holding back the truth from me—and I probably could—we're just too different. He's so inflexible." But that made her think of how hard he'd tried to be a good sport on their trip to Louisiana and how the hot peppers on his hamburger had burned his tongue and he'd tried to pretend he'd liked it. He *had* tried, she'd give him that.

But she'd tried, too.

"Puh-kin," Adam said decisively.

"What, sweetie?"

"Puh-kin!"

"Pumpkin?" Sonya suggested helpfully, which caused Adam to get very excited and launch into a loud monologue only another baby would understand.

Cindy's heart sank. That was the word Adam had been struggling for, all right. He'd been completely entranced with the pumpkin now turning orange in Luke's garden. She knew she should be excited about Adam's suddenly expanding vocabulary. But every word he'd spoken in the last few minutes—*Doggy, Luke, pumpkin*—was connected to the life they were leaving behind.

Cindy didn't sleep well that night, though Mrs. Bressler—feeling charitable after hearing that Cindy would pay for the room—had brought up a comfortable roll-away bed for her. The only thing that cheered Cindy up was the anticipation she felt at turning in her resignation at Ed's. The whole family had treated her so poorly that she felt no obligation to give them any notice. It wasn't as if they really needed her if they weren't going to follow any of her suggestions.

But when she arrived at the restaurant at 8:00 a.m., the usual time she started work, the place was dark. Her old key still fit the front door, so she went in.

"Hello? Anyone home?" Since she hadn't planned on staying, she'd brought Adam with her. Now she held on to him tightly as she walked through the dark dining room with dawning shock.

The place had been stripped and anything of value was gone, including the cash register, the fancy Fiesta dishes Ed had purchased, the red-pepper light fixtures, the silverware. The refrigerator was cleaned out—not a speck of food remained except some rotting produce. Some of the nicer pots and pans were gone and so was the marble rolling pin Manson had used to make pie crust.

Once she was sure no burglars were actually inside the restaurant with her, she picked up the phone and started to dial 9-1-1. She was interrupted, however, when she saw Margie Blankenship, who owned Tri-County Realty across the square, tapping on the glass front door and peering inside.

Margie, with her huge blond beehive and thin, thin penciled eyebrows, was the mother of the Cottonwood grapevine. Margie, if anyone, would know what was going on. Perhaps the burglary had occurred last night, and the sheriff's department—Luke—had already investigated.

She hurried to let Margie in.

"Oh, honey, I guess you didn't hear the news," Margie said excitedly. "Ed LaRue and his whole family skipped town. They took everything that wasn't nailed down and fled, just ahead of the FBI."

"FBI?"

"It seems Ed thought he could hide from the law down here. He's wanted."

"How did you find all this out?"

"Well, there was this hunky FBI agent who told me all sorts of stuff. Seems Ed is a money launderer. He sets up a bogus business, then launders Mexican drug money through it."

Cindy shook her head, amazed. "It figures Marvin would sell my café to someone like that." Now she was starting to wonder if the sale had even been legitimate. If not, she might be giving that three hundred thousand dollars right back to the FBI. She'd read about how they have the right to seize drug-deal proceeds.

Margie ran her hand along the dirty countertop. "I just hate to see the old Miracle looking so abused."

"Yeah, me, too." Cindy felt a sudden, unexpected rush of nostalgia for the old place. She longed for the smells of fresh coffee and even fresher biscuits. Funny, she hadn't even realized she'd missed them until this moment.

Now the restaurant smelled like stale mole sauce.

"I wonder what will happen to her now," Margie said, wandering behind the counter and back to the kitchen. Cindy followed her.

"I imagine the bank will foreclose on the loan, then try to sell the place."

"A body could probably pick it up for a song," Margie said idly.

"Oh, no, not me," was Cindy's immediate gut reaction. "I'm finally going to have some financial independence and some freedom. The last thing I want is to tie myself down to this place again."

"You could hire someone else to run it," Margie suggested. "Tonya. She was your right-hand girl. She would love the challenge and she needs a job real bad."

Cindy had to admit it wasn't a terrible idea.

Margie wandered into a back storage room. "Hey, look, the old neon sign."

Sure enough, there it was, leaned up against a wall. She was surprised Ed hadn't taken it. A funky vintage neon sign must be worth something.

"Oh, look, here are all the pictures." Cindy sat down on a broken chair with Adam in her lap and started fishing through the box of dusty, framed five-by-sevens that had once graced the café's walls. Some were pictures of her family, some were just vintage photos of Cottonwood. "I can't believe I just left all this stuff behind."

"You had a lot to contend with," Margie said kindly. "You know, it wouldn't be that hard to put it all back together. We could take down all that old ticky-tacky Mexican stuff and make it just like it was. I'd help you. Shoot, everyone in town would help you. Everyone's in biscuit withdrawal."

"I don't know, Margie. If I could buy it back for less than I was paid so I wouldn't be completely bankrupt again… Oh, Adam, look at this! Here's your great-great-grandmother. She's the one who invented the Miracle biscuit. Oh, and look, there's your grandpa." The picture showed Cindy's father, young and proud, standing in front of the café for its fiftieth-anniversary celebration. Cindy hadn't even been born yet.

She felt a terrible ache for both her parents.

"Here's the article *Texas Monthly* did about the café," said Margie, extracting a framed magazine article from another box. "Best biscuits in Texas. They were partial to your pecan pie, too."

"Mmm, the pecans are freshest this time of year, too," Cindy said wistfully. She'd done some cooking in the last couple of weeks, but she hadn't baked any pies or cookies or cakes. Not even any biscuits.

Adam pointed to a man in a uniform in one of the pictures. It was Deputy Potts, one of Luke's predecessors, who'd been a friend of her parents' before he'd retired.

"Luke!" Adam said excitedly.

"No, baby, that's not Luke. He's just wearing the same clothes."

"Luke. Da-da," Adam said with conviction.

"No, Luke isn't your da-da," Cindy said with equal conviction. Then she grumbled, "Lord, he probably taught you to say that when I wasn't around."

"Oh, I don't think so," Margie said. "Luke

went to considerable trouble to convince me he *wasn't* Adam's father."

"What?"

"Yeah, it was a couple of weeks ago, I guess. Not that I needed convincing. I knew that while Jim was alive, he was your one and only. But you know how rumors are."

"I never heard *that* particular rumor," Cindy said, outrage building. "Who on earth thought that?"

Margie shrugged as if it was no big deal. "Lots of people. Don't worry, I nipped it in the bud."

Cindy had forgotten about the white lie Luke had told the social worker. But for that lie, at least, she'd been extremely grateful. He'd kept Beverly Hicks from taking her child away. That all seemed like so long ago now.

"Well, thanks for sticking up for me," she said.

"Hello? Anyone home?"

Cindy didn't recognize the male voice that called out. "Back here." She got up to see who'd come in. She probably shouldn't have left the door unlocked.

Standing in the dining room was a hand-some, well-built man whose wide shoulders challenged his charcoal suit jacket. Since no one in Cottonwood wore a suit except for the undertaker, she had to assume he was from out of town. He showed a badge—FBI. Good Lord.

"Special Agent Heath Packer," he said.

"I guess I really shouldn't be in here," she stumbled. "But I work here, or I used to. I used to own it. We were just looking to see what Ed LaRue made off with."

"You must be Cindy Lefler."

"Yes, how did you know that?" She felt an instant wariness toward this serious-faced intruder.

"This is the one I was telling you about," Margie whispered in Cindy's ear. "I may have told him a little bit about you, too."

Knowing Margie, she'd told Mr. FBI Cindy's whole life story.

"You were the assistant manager here, right?" Packer asked.

"Well, for all of one week. Wait, you aren't going to hold me responsible for Ed's money laundering, are you? 'Cause I swear, the books he showed me didn't reflect any suspicious income. In fact, it looked like he was bleeding cash."

"You're not in any trouble," Packer quickly assured her. "But I need to talk to you."

"I'd love to help, but I don't know a blessed thing about Ed LaRue or his criminal dealings or where he hightailed it off to."

"Actually, I'm interested in what you can tell me about someone else."

"I've told the FBI everything I know about Marvin Carter, too. Just ask that agent in Louisiana. Del Roy? Something like that."

"I'm not interested in him, either. I was wondering if you know the whereabouts of one Brenna Thompson."

"Well, not right this second," Cindy hedged, suddenly wary. She didn't like the way this guy said Brenna's name. Handsome or not, he sounded suspicious.

"But you've seen her recently?"

About an hour ago. "We were working together trying to track down the man who swindled both of us."

"You're not exactly being forthcoming," Packer said shrewdly. "Let me ask you more directly. When was the last time you saw her, and where?"

Cindy didn't see any way out of this. "I saw her this morning. She's staying at the Kountry Kozy B and B, at the end of the block. Now would you mind telling me what you want with her?"

"Yes, I would." He turned on his heel and marched out of the café.

Cindy and Margie looked at each other. "Now what on earth do you suppose that was about?" Margie asked.

Cindy moved toward the phone. "I've got her cell number. I'm going to call her and warn her."

"You could get in trouble for that," Margie said. "If she's some kind of felon—"

"Brenna's no felon. She's an artist, a jewelry designer. I just want to make sure she's awake and not still in her pajamas." Cindy was already dialing. But she got Brenna's voice mail. Poor girl was probably still asleep. She'd stayed up half the night working on some new designs.

She hung up, picturing Brenna wearing nothing more than her teddy being startled awake by the big, bad FBI agent.

"He wasn't bad-looking," Margie said, as if she'd just read Cindy's mind. "And no wedding ring."

"No." Cindy smiled. "Brenna might give him a run for his money."

"So what do you think about restoring the Miracle Café?"

A few days ago, Cindy's answer would have

been a categorical *no.* But now she wasn't so sure. She settled into a booth with Adam in her lap, gazing at the ruined diner, remembering how it used to be—filled with customers, Kate and Iris and Tonya bustling around with their order pads and coffeepots.

The chalkboard with its daily specials. The sound of pots and pans clanging in the kitchen, orders being yelled out, Manson's good-natured grumbling.

She remembered further back, when her parents had been here, her mother running the kitchen with quiet efficiency, her father glad-handing everyone who came in, friends and strangers alike. Cindy used to sit at this very booth to do her homework, not bothered at all by the din.

She'd sat in a different booth when she and Luke had been together, the one in the back, where her mother couldn't see her so easily. She remembered sneaking bags of biscuits and corn bread for Luke to take home to Polly, whose grocery budget was always stretched to the maximum.

Cindy's memory stretched back even further, to when her grandmother had run this place. Some of the faces were different, but the feeling was always the same. Cindy's mother, waiting tables back then, had brought Cindy to work with her from the time she was a baby, just as Cindy did with Adam. Cindy could remember toddling from table to table letting the townspeople pet and admire her and how proud her mother was of her when she learned to wrap silverware packets and pour water without spilling.

If she went on the road, Adam would miss all that. Sure, he'd get a broader view of the world. He would meet people from all over, learn about different cultures, learn tolerance and flexibility and adaptability.

But he would be missing the wonders of growing up in this town. He wouldn't have a garden to dig in or a dog to romp with or a place where he could sit and do his homework or cuddle with his girlfriend while his mother was distracted. He wouldn't have his colorful circus animals near his crib to cheer him if he woke up in the night.

He wouldn't have Luke, who treated him as if he were his own flesh and blood.

Her eyes filled with tears.

"Cindy, honey, what's wrong?"

Cindy reached out and grabbed Margie's arm. "Oh, Margie, I just came so close to making a really, really big mistake. I was going to take Adam away from here."

"Well, you have to do what you have to do," Margie said, but there was a gleam in her eye, as if she'd just won a victory. "Small-town life isn't for everyone."

"I was going to take Adam away from Luke," Cindy said. "I might have thrown away the best father a kid could have."

"I'm sure you wouldn't do that," Margie said.

Cindy stood suddenly. "I have to go see him."

"But what about the diner?"

"I don't know about that yet."

Chapter Eighteen

When Cindy got to Luke's small storefront office, she discovered another deputy sitting behind Luke's desk, one she'd never even seen before. Cindy tried to pull herself together. She had to find him. She had to say what needed to be said while she was thinking clearly. "Can you tell me where Deputy Rheems is?" she asked the strange deputy.

"He, uh, well, he resigned."

"What?" How many shocks could one woman sustain in a morning?

"Well, technically he's on vacation. The sheriff told him to take a couple of weeks and think about it. But he said he wasn't coming back."

"Luke Rheems? I mean, we are talking about the same man, right?"

The deputy shrugged. "It surprised me, too. Surprised everyone. We all figured he'd be sheriff one day."

Something was terribly, terribly wrong. Cindy backed out of the office, returned to her car and drove to Luke's house, where things got even stranger. There was a Tri-County Realty For Sale sign pounded into the front yard.

This made absolutely no sense. Luke wouldn't sell his house. Had he gone completely loco?

The Blazer was here, so Luke probably was, too. Cindy unfastened Adam from his car seat and carried him inside. She started to call Luke's name, then stopped herself. What was she going to say to him? She hadn't really thought about that. She heard his voice coming from upstairs and her heart beat a little faster. She prayed it wasn't too late to fix things.

"If you can give it to me for that price, loaded," Luke was saying, "I'm prepared to come over there right now and pay cash for it."

Cash for what? Cindy wondered.

Luke's footsteps pounded down the stairs. He was carrying a large packing carton and had the cordless phone tucked between ear and shoulder.

"I can do a lot better than that down in Houston," Luke was saying, "but I'd really rather buy locally." He saw her then. His eyes widened. "Um, I'll have to call you back." He disconnected the phone and laid it down on the kitchen counter.

For several long seconds they just stared at each other. Then Adam broke the silence by stretching out his pudgy arms toward Luke. "Da-da."

Cindy quirked one eyebrow and handed Adam to Luke. Her child went so easily into Luke's arms, as if he was meant to be there. "Did you teach him to say that?"

Luke looked down. "He said it on his own, by accident I'm sure. But I sort of made a big deal of it."

"Well, at least you told me the truth."

"I plan to do that from now on."

"I would think so." She felt a little bit of her anger rearing its ugly head, but what Luke said next knocked that particular emotion right out of the water.

"I'm sorry for lying. I know it was wrong. But I plead insanity. I love you so much, Cindy, it just makes me crazy, and I was willing to do anything, even resort to subterfuge, to keep you near me. At the time, I thought I could justify it. I thought I knew best. But I was wrong. And I swear I'll never be anything but totally honest with you from now on."

He had a cowlick sticking up from his normally well-groomed hair and he looked so earnest, like a kid promising not to snitch cookies anymore, that her heart just melted.

"I'm sorry I overreacted," she said softly.

"I was planning to tell you about the money that night. That's why I was fixing you a special dinner. I wanted to be your hero. Even though I knew you'd probably leave, I was looking forward to making you happy. And I only postponed telling you because I wanted to be sure you'd get to keep the money before I got your hopes up. And, well, like I said, I wanted just a few more days to enjoy what we had going. But I knew all along it wouldn't last."

"Wait, Luke, don't say any more. Maybe it could last. I've been thinking—"

"No. I won't ask that of you. It was never fair for me to expect you to stay when your heart is set on being a world traveler."

"But, Luke—"

"I think you should go anywhere your heart

desires. But wherever you go, I'm going with you."

Now Cindy was just too stunned to speak. She couldn't have heard right. Luke wanted to travel the world with her? That's what all this was about?

"I quit my job," he continued. "I've got a lot of money saved, and I'm buying us a Winnebago, one of those medium-sized ones, you know, not the huge one but it's not dinky, either. I researched them online. I figure between my savings and yours we can travel for quite a while. Plus we'll have the proceeds on the house when it sells. Amanda Stack says I can get a lot for it, especially since we fixed up the apartment.

"And we don't always have to take the camper." He sounded more and more like an evangelist describing the road to heaven. "We can fly. I figure a trip to Europe would be good. Southern Italy is nice in the winter— I've been reading up on it."

Cindy finally found her voice. "Who are you and what have you done with Luke?"

His smile faded. "Isn't this what you wanted?"

"It's only what I thought I wanted. Oh, Luke, could any two people be more confused?" She went to him and put her arms around him, squashing Adam between them. The kid was going to have to get used to being squashed.

"I was sort of starting to like the idea of traveling," Luke said. "Are you saying you don't want to?"

"No, I do. I love traveling and I want Adam to see the world. But I also want him to have a place to call home. A house, a garden, a dog—"

"Who are you and what have you done with Cindy?"

Adam protested at being nearly smothered. Luke set him down on the kitchen floor, where he set off on his own expedition, probably looking for Doggy. Luke took Cindy back into his arms and kissed her.

"Yeah, you're Cindy, all right," he murmured. "No one else kisses like that."

"I can't believe you would give up your home for me."

"You were right all along. I *am* too inflexible, too set in my ways. I need to broaden my horizons. But it took losing you—twice—to make me see that."

She laid her head on his shoulder. "You're not the only bullheaded one. Adam isn't going to grow up some rootless nomad with no place where he feels he belongs. You just go take that sign out of your front yard right now. You aren't selling your house."

"What about the Winnebago?"

"I've sort of got my eye on this little drag-behind camper. It's small, but it would be perfect for the three of us. Well, four, counting Doggy. Weekend trips, maybe a bigger vacation once or twice a year. Mexico's not far. I've never been to Mexico."

"And what about a honeymoon? I'm still liking southern Italy, maybe Naples. And I've got a helluva lot of vacation time stacked up."

Tears sprang into Cindy's eyes. "Yes! Oh, Luke, you're crazy. I love you, and, yes, I'll marry you. But we'll have to postpone the honeymoon a couple of months. I have a little project right here in town I have to see to first."

Once Cindy got her check, she had no trouble convincing the bank that held Ed LaRue's mortgage to sell the Miracle Café property back to her. Then it was a matter of taking down all the garish Mexican décor, cleaning, repairing and replacing kitchen equipment that Ed and his family had taken with them. With practically the whole town helping, the renovation took less than a week.

All of Cindy's regular employees were ecstatic to have their old jobs back, but none was more excited than Tonya Dewhurst.

"I've been babysitting to earn a little pocket money while I looked for another job," Tonya said, "but I'll sure be glad to get a real paycheck again."

"You're getting a raise, you know," Cindy said casually.

"I am? Really? A raise? Oh, my gosh. I guess I should ask how much, but I'm just so excited I don't care. I never worked anyplace long enough before to get a raise."

"But I'll need you to take on some new responsibilities. As the manager, you'll have to open and close sometimes, handle the money, make buying decisions and—"

"Manager!" Tonya grabbed her and kissed her on the cheek. "Manager! Wait 'til I tell Mick! He'll be so proud of me!"

Cindy figured there wasn't much point in detailing Tonya's new responsibilities now, which would include running things whenever Cindy was out of town—which was going to be pretty often, the way Luke was talking. So she went back to scraping the last of the orange and yellow paint off the windows.

A workman was getting the old neon sign connected. Insta-Print had just delivered the new menus, which looked exactly like the old ones. The historic photographs had been shined up and hung on the newly painted walls. All the holes and tears in the red leatherette booths and stools had been repaired.

The food stocks had been delivered earlier that afternoon, filling the fridge and freezer and shelves with comforting stacks of flour and sugar and fresh fruits and vegetables.

It had taken nearly every penny of the three hundred thousand dollars to return everything to the way it used to be. And the little bit she had left she'd given to Brenna and Sonya so they could continue their search for Marvin. Her fellow Blondes were so grateful, they'd stayed in Cottonwood all week, scrubbing floors and painting. It was worth twelve thousand dollars and change to see Sonya on her hands and knees, wearing painter's coveralls, rubber gloves and a bandanna on her head, painting the baseboards.

Tomorrow the Miracle Café would reopen for business at 6:00 a.m. And Cindy would be there at five, rolling out that biscuit dough. She actually looked forward to it.

"Cindy?" Luke called to her from the doorway. He had an ecstatic Adam on his shoulders, doing his best to pull Luke's cap over his eyes. "I think you better come out here."

"Another problem?" she asked cheerfully as she abandoned her paint scraper and headed for the door.

What she saw out in the street brought a lump to her throat. A huge crowd of people stood in the street and spilled over into the square—the people of Cottonwood. Even Brenna and Sonya were there, carrying a big banner sign that said Welcome Back, Miracle Café.

Someone flipped a switch and the neon sign came to life, looking cleaner and brighter than it had in years. The crowd cheered. Someone even had a drum.

These people, her friends, were her greatest riches. She just hadn't appreciated them enough until now, but she would never, ever take this town or its people for granted again, no matter how far she wandered or what magnificent sights she saw.

"Speech!" someone yelled.

But she was too choked up to say a thing, and when a portable microphone was shoved in her face, she just shook her head and handed it to Luke. "You say something for me," she managed to whisper.

Luke was never at a loss for words. "I think what Cindy would like to say is thanks. Thanks for supporting the Miracle Café over all the years and now and in the future."

A cheer went up and Cindy could do nothing but grin through her tears.

When the hubbub died down and people wandered away, it was just Cindy, Luke, Adam, Sonya and Brenna in the closed restaurant, enjoying lemon meringue pie and coffee. Cindy had done a little preliminary baking and brewing to be sure all the appliances were working correctly.

"So, what happened with that FBI agent?" Cindy asked Brenna.

She shrugged. "He disappeared. Just like all the others. They say they're interested in catching Marvin, but then they don't do anything, once again leaving it up to us."

"But he wasn't interested in Marvin," Cindy pointed out. "He said very clearly his interest was in *you*."

Brenna looked a little startled. "I wonder what he meant by that?" But she didn't look displeased by the idea. In fact, she unconsciously preened, fluffing her spiky hair with one hand and using the other to toy with her silver necklace.

"So, what are your plans?" Luke asked Brenna and Sonya.

"We've been circulating Marvin's picture—the one your police-artist friend did—on the Internet," Sonya said. "We haven't said anything slanderous, just showing it around on single-women's bulletin boards, asking if anyone's seen him."

"We got a lead down in New Orleans," Brenna continued. "I thought he might end up there. We're leaving tomorrow to check it out. But not until after breakfast. After hearing about these biscuits for two weeks, we decided we can't leave Cottonwood without sampling them."

"Oh, you won't be disappointed," Luke said.

"I'll miss you guys," Cindy said, meaning it. "Remember, if you need anything just call. I want to be there when you take Marvin down. Once I get Tonya trained up a bit, I can leave anytime."

"You really like the sound of that, don't you," Luke teased her. "'I can leave any time.'"

"I do like it," she admitted. "But just because I *can* leave anytime doesn't mean I will. Not without you, anyway."

"That's all I needed to hear." He kissed her, right in front of Sonya and Brenna.

As always, Luke's kiss set her heart fluttering with an excitement, the way she felt when she was on the brink of an exciting adventure. But she also felt as if she was coming home.

* * * * *

HOMETOWN HEARTS ♥

YES! Please send me **The Hometown Hearts Collection** in Larger Print. This collection begins with 3 FREE books and 2 FREE gifts in the first shipment. Along with my 3 free books, I'll also get the next 4 books from the Hometown Hearts Collection, in LARGER PRINT, which I may either return and owe nothing, or keep for the low price of $4.99 U.S./ $5.89 CDN each plus $2.99 for shipping and handling per shipment*. If I decide to continue, about once a month for 8 months I will get 6 or 7 more books, but will only need to pay for 4. That means 2 or 3 books in every shipment will be FREE! If I decide to keep the entire collection, I'll have paid for only 32 books because 19 books are FREE! I understand that accepting the 3 free books and gifts places me under no obligation to buy anything. I can always return a shipment and cancel at any time. My free books and gifts are mine to keep no matter what I decide.

262 HCN 3432 462 HCN 3432

Name	(PLEASE PRINT)	
Address		Apt. #
City	State/Prov.	Zip/Postal Code

Signature (if under 18, a parent or guardian must sign)

Mail to the **Reader Service**:
IN U.S.A.: P.O. Box 1867, Buffalo, NY. 14240-1867
IN CANADA: P.O. Box 609, Fort Erie, Ontario L2A 5X3

Get 2 Free Books,
Plus 2 Free Gifts—
just for trying the
Reader Service!

HRLP17R

Get 2 Free Books,

Plus 2 Free Gifts—

just for trying the Reader Service!

Get 2 Free Books,
Plus 2 Free Gifts—
just for trying the Reader Service!

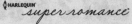 Harlequin super romance

Get 2 Free Books,
Plus 2 Free Gifts—
just for trying the Reader Service!

HARLEQUIN
HEARTWARMING™

Get 2 Free Books,
Plus 2 Free Gifts -
just for trying the *Reader Service!*

Get 2 Free Books,
Plus 2 Free Gifts—
just for trying the
Reader Service!

READERSERVICE.COM

Manage your account online!
- Review your order history
- Manage your payments
- Update your address

> **We've designed the**
> **Reader Service website**
> **just for you.**

Enjoy all the features!
- Discover new series available to you, and read excerpts from any series.
- Respond to mailings and special monthly offers.
- Browse the Bonus Bucks catalog and online-only exculsives.
- Share your feedback.

Visit us at:

ReaderService.com